Chrysanthemum Ben.

A Story.

The sole intellectual rights of this original work belong to the author

All rights are reserved. No part of this work may be reproduced, stored in a retrieval system, or transmitted in any form or by any means, without the prior permission of the author.
This work is a Historical Drama and names of real people (now all deceased) have been used.

All conversations, actions and events are fictional.

Chapter 1.

It was November 1932. His Excellency The Emperor Hirohito had summoned his brothers and male cousins to the small room in the Imperial palace. Winter was beginning to bite, there had been flurries of snow but the noon sun had sent it away.

"Why are we here? What's this about?" Prince Takeda spoke quietly to his uncle Chichibu. It wasn't a whisper but the silence and acoustics in the ornately panelled room lit by the weakening winter sun amplified his voice.

"Don't know, but according to the servants and courtiers he spends most of his days studying the teachings of Nichiren."

"Is that good or bad do you think?"

"Not sure. Nichiren was pretty revolutionary in his time. He taught that enlightenment could be achieved in this world. That would correspond with the Emperors vision of himself."

"Do you think he really believes he's enlightened? A God?"

"Not sure, he's so detached from reality that he may. Everyone and everything in his life act as though he is, so it must be hard to think that you aren't."

"Is there anything you're sure about?"

"No. but I wish he'd stuck to Marine Biology and not adopted Nichiren."

Prince Yaswhiko Asaka the Emperor's brother sat on his own the other side of the room sitting quietly on the thin legged chair. There were seven people in the ornate room. The three brothers, Mikasa Takamatsu and Chichibu, three male cousins, Takeda, Tarama, Otowa. The floors were highly polished cedar block parquet in a diamond pattern. The furniture and soft furnishings in 'French' style. Elegant thin slim curved legs supported the chairs and occasional tables. Heavy yellow to gold curtains draped the windows. Chandeliers hung from an ornately panelled ceiling. The room centred on a 'Shinto' shrine on the end wall. The chilling cold still managed to creep into the room.

"Asaka is not well, I can smell the wine from here." Chichibu commented.

"Do you think His Excellency knows?"

"I'm not sure but he can't hide it today."

A soft gong sounded outside the room. The double doors to the left of the shrine were silently opened by kneeling servants, their eyes riveted to the floor. Only the Emperor used this door.

Emperor Hirohito entered the room. Those that were sitting stood up, another soft gong sounded and the doors closed. The formal Kimono like, regal yellow Sokutai made him look bigger than he was. The stiff material belled out hiding his feet. The large wing like shoulders tapered to his waist, a false vertical hairpiece rose from the top of his head making him look taller. His thick lensed gold framed glasses almost seemed part of the ornate uniform.

There was no introduction or welcome from the Emperor, he moved and stood in front of the shrine. There was a serious silence, just the rustle of fabric. Chichibu coughed into his handkerchief.

"Today is the start of the biggest task Japan will ever undertake." His voice was light, whatever he said could not be questioned. He was the Emperor.

"Japan and the world will follow the directives of the great monk Nichiren who now speaks through me.

'Enlightenment can be achieved in this world. Social and political peace are dependant on the quality of the belief system that is upheld in a nation.'

It is our, and thus your duty to give the world our beliefs, our values, our social and political fabric. It is for the betterment of the world.

To achieve that we must protect, conquer and control the world. That is your task.

Japan has few natural resources, it's greatest power is the strength of it's people stiffened by their allegiance to this throne. The Chrysanthemum Throne.

'I will never yield. All other troubles are no more to me than dust before the wind. I will be the Pillar of Japan. I will be the eyes of Japan. I will be the great ship of Japan. This is my vow and I will never forsake it.'"

The Emperor paused as if giving time for his message to be understood.

"Now we protect only Korea, that will change, you will change it. To do that we need the things that the lower world values. Gold, silver, platinum, any precious metal, any gem, any coin, any banknote. These are things that will not be relevant to their lives. At this time their lives are not relevant. Japan and the enrichment of this throne is all that is relevant. Our military must grow, we must conquer and control in order to obtain the means to make this throne the most powerful and rich house in the world, only then we can enlighten the world."

The Emperor looked around the room, his eyes connecting with every individual in the room.

"You will do that. Start with Korea, strip it of anything of value, send our armies into every bank vault, every pagoda, every house every piece of art, every ancient manuscript, anything with value. Use it to build our armies then unleash them on the drug soaked turmoil of China. It has everything we need for our task.

Remember we cannot fail. To fail is death."

The soft gong sounded again, the doors swung open and the emperor left.

"What on earth does that mean?" Takeda whispered to Chichibu.

"It means millions will die. It means our generals will be very happy, it means many mothers will shed many tears. The Emperor wants the world and everything in it."

Chapter 2.

The white ship resolutely forced aside the heavy rolling soup of the South China Sea. It's middle funnel discharging acrid dark smoke, the two other funnels, impostors, clean and dysfunctional. Their purpose merely to assist the large green cross painted on each side of the hull. A floating deception of the worst moral and ethical kind. A treasure ship disguised as a hospital.

Only a few hours before, during the first light of the day, the Huzi Maru had inched slowly away from the Saigon wharf. Prince Takeda had stood on the stern looking at the platforms of stout green mangroves that floated quickly passed. Dark green rafts that captured the human detritus of Saigon. He knew he had looked into his last human eyes for some time. The bogus ship, crewed by Japanese sailors all knew his royal status. The red and gold fourteen petal flower on his white robes created an uncrossable void between him and lesser humanity. He had passed the last week with his uncle Prince Chichibu counting on the heavy bronze and wooden crates as they were hoisted and portered aboard. Chichibu was ill. Struck down by tuberculosis ten years ago, he had never fully recovered and was supposed to be living in the clear mountain air at the foot of Mount Fuji. Yet here he was, with blood stained handkerchiefs in the hot, wet, reeking air of Saigon.

The Japanese forces had been ruthless and successful in their real agenda, the theft of gold and valuables from occupied countries. Hirohito's lie was that the occupation was for Asian countries to come together and unite with Japan to free themselves from the yoke of colonialism. It was an easier message than his mission to impose on the world the teachings of an ancient Japanese monk.

The acquisition at gunpoint of all their wealth, had a name. Operation 'Golden Lily' named after one of Hirohito's poems. All male members of the 'Chrysanthemum Throne' had been given deadly responsibilities that required them to have no regard for human life in their execution. Indeed the regular taking of human lives was an encouraged strategy to frighten occupied populations. Chichibu was the 'collector'. Takeda the 'tally man'.

His mind had wandered and flitted to the scurrying coolies on the wharf side, dressed in dirty shorts and bamboo hats. They let go, pulled in and coiled the stout sun aged, almost white ropes that had tethered the ship to the shore whilst it was being laden with stolen gold, stolen silver, stolen diamonds and gems. A million glittering love laden memories ruthlessly prised from their settings and their owners. It did not matter. All that mattered was that Japan and the Emperor were great. The greater the better, but to do that it needed oil, guns, bombs, ships, planes. It needed money and gold was money in its purest form. His gaze had moved over the dark swirling water, the mangrove clumps were now not racing towards the sea but almost motionless as the tide peaked and stopped the Saigon river in its timeless tracks. Beyond the wharf were tall thin houses. A disarray of heights, colours and sizes, he could see a little girl on the roof, she wore a yellow dress and skipped about from here to there doing this and that, her pure and untainted imagination creating real worlds in which she happily played. It made him think of his beautiful wife Mitsuko and their little son who was soon to be one year old and with whom he had enjoyed so little time.

Two sailors quickly moved passed him and wrenched him back to now, walking in almost a bowing stance with eyes riveted to the dull red painted metal deck. They were human just like him, he thought, but not like him, the relative of a living god.

The occupation of French Indochina in the summer of 1940 had been hot but easy. The French had capitulated and had been allowed to maintain a facade of colonial control whilst paying over all resources and monies to Japanese commanders. It was a good deal, the French already had in place the mechanisms of colonial extortion so why replace it? Chichibu and his men had been thorough, moving from town to town looting banks shops and homes. The deaths simply served as a reminder of the terrible stories and terrifying reputation the Japanese army had gained at Nanking in 1937. By early June there was enough gold bullion to fill the ship.

The last night had been pleasant, dining and relaxing with Chichibu in the old wooden presidential palace. The last gasp rains of the wet season had cooled the evening air and had stimulated the frogs and crickets to fill the night with a croaking rasping choir. Although the food had been Vietnamese it was tolerable and the French wine helped to assuage the evening . Their conversation intruded well into the night talking to each other, looking at each other's faces, matching his face to his words, smiling, laughing, sadness as they spoke of families and children. But now it had gone.

There was now no land to be seen. His gloved hand reached for the simple door latch on the starboard bridge door. It was a dull grey sky that shaded the sea to greys and deep greens. He entered onto the bridge, the officers immediately bowed and focused their gaze downward.

Captain Toichi was engrossed in maps on the large wooden table at the rear of the bridge. He had not noticed Prince Takeda enter.

"Yes Captain I am here. What is it you want?"

Captain Toichi snapped to attention with a respectful click of his heels and focused his gaze on the red emblem.

"Your Excellency, please accompany me into my day cabin."

The immaculately uniformed captain took off his glasses, bowed and opened the door to his day cabin. It was small, clad in wood with a comfortable bunk, a table and two wooden chairs upholstered in dark green velvet. Toichi quickly moved around the table and pulled out one of the chairs.

"Your Excellency please sit down."

Toichi remained standing, almost to attention.

"Sir, about a year ago in November last year a German raider called Atlantis captured an English converted merchant ship called 'Automedon'. On board were many things of great interest including all the codes and ships call signs for Great Britain and its allies operating in the Pacific and Asian regions. As you are aware Germany and ourselves have been sharing information since the pact of 1936 and so we have been able to decode enemy signals."

"Yes?"

"Would you like some tea Sir?"

"No, please go on."

"I have received a signal from Tokyo saying that our spies in Singapore have reported that two Dutch submarines, manned by British crews have been loaded and indeed overloaded with large amounts of gold and silver bullion. They believe this bullion to be from Hong Kong, the British moved large amounts of bullion in 1939 to Singapore believing it to be safe."

"Yes yes, go on."

"You must understand Sir that this is Japanese intelligence and has not been shared with our German allies."

Takeda looked bemused but still Toichi resolutely centered his eyes on the red emblem, picking up his bemusement only with his peripheral vision.

"So why are you telling me this?"

"German intelligence has signaled that one of their targets, the cruiser HMAS Sydney has recently left Fremantle port and is tasked with escort duties. The Germans have dispatched one of their surface raiders - the Kormoran - to intercept the cruiser, engage it and sink it. It is simply a military engagement for the Germans".

"All very well Captain but our job, or rather my job is to get this cargo safely to Tokyo."

"I'm sorry Sir but Tokyo wish you to be aware of these facts and for you to make a decision. I will of course obey your Excellency's commands."

Takeda made himself more comfortable stretching out his legs to the side of the table, the legs of the wooden chair scraped on the metal deck.

"Our intelligence from Australia and Hong Kong is that HMAS Sydney has been used many times to move bullion from Hong Kong to both Singapore and Australia. Tokyo is of the opinion that Sydney's real mission is to rendezvous with the two submarines and transfer the bullion for safe receipt in Australia."

"Captain, we are effectively an unarmed hospital ship what are we supposed to do with all this intelligence, information and supposition?"

"Sir, Tokyo suggests that we steam towards the general area of the Kormoran Sydney intercept and just see what happens. They say that the amount of bullion involved is so much that we should at least consider something."

"And where is the intercept area?"

"The Germans are aiming for an area about three hundred miles off the eastern coast of Australia."

"The exact opposite direction to which we are currently heading. And the Germans gave us this information?"

"No Sir we've broken their codes."

"Have the Germans any idea there is bullion involved?"

"No Sir, it's just a military target to them."

Takeda rocked back in the chair.

"What would you do Captain Toichi?" Takeda asked addressing him by his name for the first time. This immediately affected Toichi who pulled out the second chair and sat down elevating his gaze from the emblem to his throat.

"Sir, I am the chauffeur, you own the car. I cannot, dare not, advise you."

"We will have some tea Captain."

"Yes Sir." Toichi rose and pulled the small wooden handle on the bulkhead.

The tea was the perfect temperature, as though the steward had been nursing it in anticipation. The silence went on and on.

"Captain how long will it take to make that area?"

"About two to three days Sir."

"And do we have any armaments at all?"

"Yes Sir, we have ten machine guns, five either side, they're concealed by white painted boards but there are slits for them to fire through."

"And do we have anybody who can fire them?"

"Yes Sir, we have a platoon of thirty fully trained soldiers onboard to protect the cargo. You wouldn't know as they're dressed as sailors."

"Have we got enough fuel, water, provisions to accomplish this diversion?"

"Yes Sir."

Takeda got up and paused at the door.

"Captain, logic tells me that I am putting this ship and it's cargo at an unnecessary risk for something that I really can't justify, but nevertheless Tokyo and thus the Emperor deems it important enough to provide me with the option and I will feel cowardly if I do not comply with his wishes. Please alter course for the intercept area."

"Yes Sir." Toichi clicked his heels and saluted.

Takeda stopped and looked at the oil smooth sea as he left the bridge. He felt so alone. Oh to laugh and giggle with his baby boy.

Chapter 3

The dark velvet nights always succumbed to the irresistible power of the rising sun, changing the black water to deep dark greens, or playful blues depending on where he stood. Wherever he stood he was alone, no one dared to approach him save to answer his spoken requests, they were always considered a direct order coming from the highest authority. Today there was a wind that changed the sea from its oil smoothness to dancing girls with diamonds in their hair.

Captain Toichi approached from behind him and announced his presence with the click of his heels, followed by the obligatory bow.

"Your Excellency, we have been searching the intercept area for two days and I have to manage the ship's resources, could you inform me of your further requirements?"

Takeda stared out over the stern his white loose uniform snapped and cracked in the wind at the green painted stanchions.

"Yes Captain I think we have done our best, no sightings or contact by noon and we turn and head for Tokyo."

"Yes Sir. I agree you have made a valiant effort considering that we have no explicit orders and no means to engage an enemy."

Captain Toichi said his words staring at Prince Takeda's neck.

"Ahoy there! Smoke on the horizon, port forward bow." The shout drifted down from the duty sailor in the crow's nest, his large long binoculars pinpointing and seeing the black smoke that was invisible to Takeda and Toichi.

"Your instructions Sir?" Toichi asked.

"Alter course Captain."

"Where to Sir. The smoke or Tokyo?"

Takeda turned away, leaning on the stern rail he gazed for a moment at the surging parcels of water being pushed by the ship's propeller. After an age, he spoke.

"The smoke Captain, the smoke."

Toichi clicked his heels in acknowledgement and turned to go.

"Captain how long will it take us to reach the smoke?"

"It's on the far horizon Sir, so I would estimate about three hours."

"As fast as you can Captain please, I want to finish this quickly."

"Yes Sir."

Takeda lay on his bed in his cabin, the bed consisted of teak slabs at least six inches thick, over six foot long and three foot wide. There were three sections that followed him everywhere, it took six of his staff to lift one section. He was alone staring at the brass scuttle watching the horizon gently appear and disappear as the ship throbbed its way towards the smoke. A knock came at the metal door. A folded paper slid under the gap at the bottom. He read the note and made his way up to the bridge.

All heads bowed as he entered. All conversation stopped as he entered. Captain Toichi was not on the bridge, a white gloved hand gestured towards the day cabin. The hand opened the door. Toichi was pouring over the maps and signals on the table. He clicked to attention and immediately shut the cabin door.

"Your Excellency, the lookout has spotted four lifeboats about two miles away, off the starboard bow. They're German boats so that means that the Kormoran has sunk and the smoke is most probably a damaged 'Sydney'. I am obliged to rescue them and then we will proceed towards the smoke." Captain Toichi conveyed his message hoping that the routine procedure outlined to Takeda would be accepted and not challenged. It was unforgivable not to rescue fellow mariners.

There was no delay Takeda responded immediately.

"There will be no stopping or slowing captain. Instruct your officers they are to ignore all distress signals and to make full progress towards the Sydney."

Toichi's eyes momentarily strayed for an instant to the face of Takeda then instantly dropped. Not speaking he left the cabin and instructed the Bridge Officers to make full way towards the smoke with no stopping. The silence on the bridge was now made heavy with human guilt.

After fifteen minutes the white painted ship rushed by leaving the small open lifeboats bobbing furiously in her wake. The German sailors demeanour having gone from happy relief to incredulous dismay as they realized the 'Huzi Maru' had left them to their fate, left them to die. Their shouts became fainter as the distance broadened, some officers and crew risked a backward guilt laden glance. They were now far enough away not to see their eyes.

It was nothing to Takeda, he hadn't watched them die, they may make it, they weren't that far off the Australian coast and according to Toichi's maps the current was in that direction. He had watched men die before. Chinese prisoners in Manchuria had been gassed in a compound of the infamous unit 731. He was known at that time as Lieutenant Colonel

Miyata and held a financial executive post for the unit and so had been invited to observe the progress the chemists had made. A green yellow mist rolling over unsuspecting humans, the frantic search for escape once the realization set in. The convulsions and wretched anguish settling into occasional twitches and jerks that seemed to go on and on as the fight for life was lost. The vision was in his mind for life but his obligations to Hirohito were bigger than life itself.

"What are your plans and orders Sir when we reach the Sydney?" Toichi asked the question on the bridge in full hearing of his officers.

"At the moment I have none, we will see what we will see and go from there."

"I estimate we are about thirty minutes steaming from the ship. Do you have any immediate orders Your Excellency?"

Takeda stared resolutely at the now clearly visible smoke.

" Captain, have your men stand to at the machines guns on both sides, and ensure they have plenty of ammunition."

There was a small pause before Toichi issued his order. A Junior Officer quickly left the bridge, bowing as he went.

The silence on the bridge simply added to Takeda's undisclosed sorrow so he left and stood outside looking at the sky, the sea anything but the crew.

The sorrow had started to build after 731, the human anguish indelible, the awful sounds visited him most nights. The fact that his staff who surrounded him at the time all had to show approval at the dreadful things happening in front of their eyes, separated only by wire and sealed glass. One side life, one side death. It was more than a job, it was the wishes of the Emperor as interpreted by men. His wishes had to be fulfilled. Then there had been Nanking in thirty seven. The Emperor had put his drunken uncle Prince Asaka in charge, the Japanese army had simply been let loose on the Chinese population and the worst type of group madness had prevailed. Murder usually followed rape, rape was ubiquitous, women old and young, female children and ageing grandmothers all suffered and died, usually on the end of a bayonet or sharpened bamboo stakes.

He had arrived there in early February 1938 and witnessed piles of rotting stinking corpses being shoved into the river. He had turned away and avoided the sights, the smells, the constant screaming as something terrible nearby happened. He had concentrated on the pure accounting of all the loot Chichibu had collected. Chichibu was a heavy drinker who never got drunk. It was as a panacea of all the evil wrongs that were around him, surrounded him, choked him until he stopped seeing. His TB a small sufferance gladly suffered compared to the horror around him.

"Sir, the Sydney is in sight." Captain Toichi had left the bridge and was now beside him. He handed him a pair of binoculars. Takeda brought them up to his eyes.

"It's listing heavily to port and on fire, do you think it's making way or just drifting Toichi?"

The captain moved closer to the prince.

"I think it's just drifting Sir. There's no wake and all the crew are on deck, they're not shipping lifeboats so I don't think it's in danger of sinking."

"How long until we're alongside?"

"About fifteen minutes Sir."

"Good, approach starboard side on from the stern, close enough for boarding parties."

"Yes Sir."

"Captain Toichi." Takeda turned and looked directly at Toichi's small round face.

"Ready the gun crews on the starboard side and on my order open fire. There are to be no survivors, do you understand me."

Toichi rocked slightly back on his heels as in the silence he processed the terrible command. Without a word he turned and went back onto the bridge. After a moment another junior officer left the bridge.

Takeda stood alone as the two ships neared. He could see and hear the crew cheering and waving, jumping up and down, some of them with blood stained limbs, some of them with blood stained dressings . The relief was palpable as the white ship with a green cross closed on them. The flames could still be seen licking out of a hole in the stern and from a forward gun turret. A large dirty oil slick slowly followed her drifting journey. Takeda entered the bridge and stood alongside Toichi whose frozen face showed no sign of emotion. The Huzi Maru was now inching forward matching the speed of the drifting grey and black warship until they were level, only twenty meters apart.

Takeda looked at Toichi and nodded. Toichi paused then spoke quickly and harshly into the brightly polished brass voice pipe. Instantly the concealed machine guns opened fire through the small slits in the white painted boards. The noise banged between the hulls, the cacophony melding into almost a propeller like throbbing. He could see and hear the bullets zipping and thudding into the bodies and heads of the sailors. They had no time to run or hide. It was a simple massacre. After three minutes there were no signs of movement or life on the slanted deck of HMAS Sydney. The guns stopped one by one until the ocean took over the sound. Blood was everywhere, bodies had fallen into the sea and had drifted into the dirty oil that instantly covered them in black unnatural slime. Dead hands clung on to lower rails, trails of blood flowed down the inclined damaged deck to drip into the close by sea. It was a scene of utter destruction somehow made surreal by the dancing sun and the blue warm ocean.

"Captain, please send over boarding parties, search the ship for any survivors and remove them, survey the damage and estimate how long the ship will remain afloat. Locate any bullion that may be onboard. I will be in my cabin. Please remember, no survivors." Takeda didn't wait for a response for he knew that any response would somehow be tinged with utter contempt and disgust at what he was forcing the captain to do. He lay on his bed even more alone than one hour ago. Then, he could address Toichi by his name and it would draw them together. Now he was alone again. He closed his eyes and tried to sleep but no sleep came, only the past and now this awful present came to compound his sorrow.

For the first time Captain Toichi knocked on Takeda's cabin door. It was opened by his servant, a small subservient Japanese man in his mid thirties who beckoned Captain Toichi in but made no sound. Toichi clicked and bowed to awaken the slumbering Prince. Takeda opened his eyes, they were not dulled by sleep, he didn't have to focus or rub, his eyes had been shut but there had been no sleep. He pulled himself up and gestured Toichi to sit alongside him on the bed. Toichi remained standing stiffly to attention. the servant noiselessly floated outside of the large cabin.

"Sir I have to report that there are no survivors, the ship has been searched , I have been onboard myself and in my estimation the ship is no danger of imminent sinking. All the watertight doors to the damaged sections are holding and the fires have been extinguished."

"And the gold captain, is there any gold?"

"Your Excellency there is a considerable amount of what appears to be gold and silver bullion, all in seventy five kilo bars packed four to a crate. Some crates are metal some are wood. We cannot check beyond the damaged areas ."

"Instruct all your men to get it onboard as soon as possible Captain then when it's done set charges and sink it." Takeda thought as he looked at the grey and black bobbing hull through the scuttle.

"How long will it take Captain?"

"I would think about two days Sir. We are fully loaded already and we'll have to stow it in unusual places."

"Have your sailors ship it aboard Captain. Arrange shifts to work through the night and order the soldiers to have their arms at the ready to guard the sailors, I don't want anything to go missing. I'll be along shortly to start inventorying."

Toichi saluted and left, the cabin door swung open for him as he approached.

The two ships were now connected by a rudimentary moving gangplank. Takeda instructed the junior officer to rig side ropes on the gangplank fearing that bullion may be lost over the side as the two vessels jostled and rubbed uneasily together. He insisted that every crate be opened as it was lugged unceremoniously onto the dull red painted deck. Every now and then a black slimy corpse would bounce between the hulls then slide away. Face down, bobbing gently as it slowly moved down between the two ships that occasionally came together and crushed it. The crack of the ribs could be clearly heard. It warranted no response.

After eighteen hours Takeda summoned Toichi to relieve him, whilst he ate and slept. His mind was beginning to dull with fatigue and he feared making a mistake. He could see that Captain Toichi resented this imposed task but he said nothing. In his cabin, this time, sleep came quickly.

The two conjoined ships rubbed together for two and a half days before Captain Toichi reported that all the bullion had been transferred.

"What about the damaged sections Captain. Have we searched those section?"

Takeda could see that Toichi was weary, his usual crispness had been blunted by the long hours, he needed a shave and was not wearing his cap.

Toichi exhaled, almost a sigh. "Sir, I consider it too dangerous for my crew to enter those areas."

Takeda placed both his hands on the guard rail and gazed at the damaged hulk, he estimated about thirty percent of the ship had not been accessed. He said nothing for several minutes, the light was diminishing as the orange sun dived towards the western horizon. The thought passed through his mind that it always seemed that dramatic powerful moments such as sunrise and sunset somehow made your thoughts deeper. More philosophical!

Turning to Toichi he said. "Set charges and sink it Captain then set course for Tokyo."

Captain Toichi saluted but did not click. After an hour the Australian cruiser HMAS Sydney slowly drifted away from the Huzi. Captain Toichi remained on the bridge, Takeda located himself on the forecastle then at exactly eight o'clock there came a sound, a muffled 'crump', a few rockets of flame then the cruiser slid quickly stern first into the blackness of the warm watery night. The Huzi shuddered as the propeller bit into that same water then once underway heeled over to starboard as it changed course.

Takeda made his way aft to his cabin, the cooling breeze increased in line with the ship's speed, his noiseless valet sprang up and opened the door. Takeda dismissed him and closed the door himself. He was alone, another day had passed without one single sight of a human eye. His thoughts amended that, of course he had seen eyes but none had looked into his.

Thoughts queued up in his head as he lay down. The thud of bullets going into people who, seconds earlier were jumping for joy as the white ship approached their burning hulk. The awful gentle bobbing of black slime bodies that floated and moved with the wind and sea. The looks of hopeful desperation that turned to dreadful realization as the Huzi steamed past the struggling survivors of the Kormoran. The flattened gasping horrible contortions of dying faces slowly sliding down the glass windows of 731. The endless gold bars, four to a box, so heavy it took six men to lift and move them. In his logic he struggled to relate the heavy dour metal with life itself, how the whole world somehow lived and died for it. Why?

If there was no gold what would humanity use as a measure of superiority? These were very dangerous thoughts that kept leading him to more and more questions. Better to seek comfortable refuge in that the Emperor would be pleased about the amount of additional gold and silver he had acquired. He knew deep down it wasn't even for Japan. It was simply to make the Chrysanthemum Throne the richest and most powerful in the world. Paper money was simply that - paper - but gold and silver; well that was indestructible for all known time. Sleep would be an elusive fairy tonight. Maybe after some time, after some space from this ship, after he'd done his duty with Mitsuko sleep would come.

Chapter 4.

It was a duty, set in the peace and tranquility of their home, surrounded by beauty, trees and flowers. Takeda and Mitsuko spent time with their son whilst palace servants hovered. At night she was dutiful and passive. In the morning he was active. There was fondness and tenderness but not passion. The reputation of their ancestors lay with them. Genealogy imposed formidable expectations on their performance. far more important than love. Love was for songs, poetry and teenage girls.

Takeda grew closer to his son as he watched him discover the world. So much to know, so much to learn. Just so much. Mitsuko watched Takeda watching their son. She knew that playing his games, pretending to laugh at the things he laughed at removed her husband from his awful life. The only thing she knew about his life was that it was awful. The Emperor had the vision, he didn't know about misery, pain, loss, destruction, or death. No one dared to tell him. Their ancestors performance was measured by today's gold.

She knew that when the Emperor's brother Prince Chichibu came to the house her husband would soon leave. Leave her, leave their son, leave their home, leave her pregnant.

Chichibu and Takeda walked with Emperor Hirohito in the warm spring sun. A wave of cherry blossom was sweeping up from the south but was still one or two days away from the gardens of the palace. The trees were impatient to display their delicate moist new flowers The spring sun teased them to blossom. Ten meters behind was a small entourage of courtiers silently carrying water, a towel, a glass, an umbrella, a coat, a notebook. He was dressed in a western style light grey suit. He was the sovereign of the state, the head of the military. A living God. It was a pretence that his role was perfunctory or symbolic.

Most days he walked in the garden, when he was alone he constantly chanted Nichiren's mantra 'Nam Myoho Renge Kyo'.

"----- We must focus on this world, *Individual empowerment and inner transformation contribute to a better and more peaceful world*. So we must do our best to control the world. To make this happen.

When a tree has been transplanted, though fierce winds may blow, it will not topple if it has a firm stake to hold it up. But even a tree that has grown up in place may fall over if its roots are weak. Even a feeble person will not stumble if those supporting him are strong, but a person of considerable strength, when alone, may fall down on an uneven path.

Japan will be the stake for the world, we will support the world. China and Asia must give us their wealth so we can do this. You will follow and direct our armies to do this. The Chrysanthemum Throne must bring peace in this world. However difficult that is.---------"

Chichibu and Takeda bowed as the Emperor left them and moved towards the heavy wooden doors. They swung quietly open as he approached. He stopped, turned and spoke.

"Prince Takeda, Prince Chichibu, you will go to Haiphong and Hanoi, make sure the Chinese do not get arms or support into Southern China. Make sure the French are cooperating with our Generals and strip the north of French Indo China of all the gold you can find. Chichibu, you move on to Singapore as soon as it's ours. General Yamashita will be heading the armies moving down Malaya so I should think it won't be long, early next year. Our spies report that the British have moved large amounts of gold from Hong Kong to Singapore for safe keeping just before we took Hong Kong. The Dutch and British have moved most of their gold bullion reserves to Jakarta and Singapore because of the European war. So we must be thorough. Chichibu you must obtain, Takeda you must inventorise and ship back to Tokyo. I cannot trust my Generals. I can only trust blood relatives of the throne and so you may not have much time for your families."

It was a factual statement, not an apology. The Emperor turned and entered the doors. The entourage scurried in quickly behind him just before the great doors closed.

Chapter 5.

The voyage from Jakarta had been uncertain. The bogus ship had been destined for Tokyo but a signal had diverted them to Luzon in the Philippines due to American submarine activity in the waters around Japan.

It took four worrying but uneventful days to sight Luzon. The sea had been calm and the weather benign but he knew Captain Sagawaga was nervous that allied submarines and surface warships would see through the white paint or that the radio codes had been changed. The Captain had not communicated with him during this time, there had been no reason to, he was doing his job and that had limits but now those limits were convenient. In fact Takeda had spoken to no one for four days and nights other than issue orders and requirements to his valet who always responded with efficacy and perfection but no sound.

Captain Sagawaga 'clicked' behind him as he leant on the rail. The Huzi was cutting slowly across the top of Lingayen gulf, the landmass of San Fernando Port was now clearly visible as the flotsam of human habitation began to appear. A broken wooden crate bounced off the starboard hull before bobbing away in the wake, the odd rotting coconut moved pointlessly in the presiding current, a dirty glass bottle continued its watery journey.

" We will be docking in San Fernando in about an hour Sir. What are your instructions?"

"Secure the ship alongside Captain, then instruct all your crew to remain below deck out of sight. We will be met by Colonel Adachi and a contingent of soldiers who will unload the cargo. When that is completed I will leave your ship and you can carry on with your orders."

"That will take several days Sir."

"Not if the soldiers work through the night. I would estimate about thirty six hours."

Sagawaga saluted again and turned to leave.

"Captain!"

Sagawaga stopped in his tracks but didn't turn.

"I shall mention your unquestioning patriotism to the Emperor when I next see him."

Sagawaga turned, stiffened to attention and once again saluted towards the red flower on Takeda's tunic. He said nothing, then stiffly marched away, his shoes resounding on the metal deck. Turning back to the rail the single pier of San Fernando Port was now clearly visible, jutting out into the dark deep water of the bay waiting for the Huzi Maru to inch her way towards the forty dark green army trucks lined up a two abreast on the quayside.

It was the first time Takeda had set foot on occupied Philippine soil. Ever since Pearl Harbour The Americans had vastly increased their naval presence, they had lost several treasure ships to hunting submarines, only the bogus hospital ships were safe and now even that was not a certainty. The Emperor had decreed that all the remaining treasure be hidden underground in the Philippines as a safeguard should the war be lost. That day in 1942 he chose to travel in an ox cart rather than a staff car so that he could smell and absorb the country into his body and mind. His entourage and military escorts on that day had been astounded at his action but totally subservient in their acceptance.

The convoy of foot soldiers, staff cars and three military trucks had made agonizingly slow progress behind the shuffling oxcart guided by a nervous foot soldiers more used to a motorbike or armoured car. Colonel Adachi had sat at his side. Takeda in pristine white that made the deep red and gold chrysanthemum emblem almost glow in the gentle morning sun. The colonel, nervous, agitated and quiet, not knowing what to say in the awkward alien situation, constantly but quietly tapped his pace stick against the stiff leather calf of his shiny brown boots. Takeda, oblivious to any existence below him looked and took in the dirt road. It was early in the morning, a light shower with heavy raindrops had mottled the dry dirt into a mosaic decorated by footprints and wheel tacks. He could still smell the heavy water as it moved away. The jolting of the cart, the smell of the pulling beasts and the sounds of Philippino life reached him through the filtering palms and jungle. His mission was huge, his resources were huge, he had over a thousand men, engineers, explosives experts, electricians, architects, miners, ceramic and concrete experts, access to unlimited labour. Philippino peasants, Korean labourers forcibly shipped in along with their 'Comfort Women' to keep the Japanese soldiers happy, prisoners of war from every continent, all of them were in reality expendable slaves. His orders too horrific, too brutal and too much for him to think about as the cart stopped at Adachi's bidding.

Takeda looked to his right, two peasants were labouring in the field, one old, one young, they were intentionally engrossed in cutting cane, not daring to look up to the road and the strange Japanese convoy that had stopped on it. Adachi summoned a foot soldier to him and spoke in a soft lilting voice that was totally at odds with his harsh physical presence.

The foot soldier was almost quivering in front of Adachi, his gaze low and submissive as though the unavoidable road dirt on his boots was an insult to his Colonel. After a few seconds the soldier paced backwards one pace and deftly withdrew the long bayonet, fixing it to the muzzle of his rifle with only two sounds, the clunk of metal on metal and the click of the spring as it located. The soldier turned and jumped into the low wet ditch that bordered the road, springing through it and into the cane field without thought to the wet green sludge that soaked immediately into his boots and fatigues.

The soldier's almost screaming shouts were unavoidable, the two peasants stopped hacking at the cane, their bolos hung at their sides as the frantic soldier stormed up, the bayonet and rifle pointed waist height at them. The muzzle pointed towards the young youth then waved towards the road as the soldier grunted in Japanese.

It was obvious what the soldier wanted Ben to do.

Ben was seventeen, brown and lean with the perfection of youth, a beautiful star eyed face was simply adorned with an illuminating broad smile that revealed perfect white teeth. He glanced nervously towards his uncle who was standing motionless beside the uncut cane. His uncle's eyes were riveted on the muzzle of the gun that waved between Ben and the road.

After motionless seconds the soldier shouted at Ben to move, the language was strange but the meaning was clear. Ben's uncle nodded that he should go.

Ben's heart was beating fast, thumping in his chest, not with exertion but with fear. He walked towards the ditch knowing that a bayonet and a bullet were pointing at his back. He wondered what it would feel like to be killed by a long sharp metal knife pushed into your back, would it be no more than a cut with the sharp hard blade, once in, cutting painlessly inside him, would he feel it sawing and dissecting inside his body? How long would it take to die? Would the soldier pull it out? Of course he would, it was part of his rifle.

Was this it? Why did they want a poor peasant worker? What possible use could he be? Yes they were going to kill him, probably as an example to others. Yes that was it, his uncle would see and tell everyone in the village. He didn't notice the ditch or the effort to climb out of it the other side. The soldier pushed him towards an ox cart at the head of the military convoy. So many guns, how were they going to do it? Perhaps they would slit his throat and let him die in the dust of the road, blood sprayed by the last frantic pumps of his heart. A bullet in the back of his head would be quick. By now his whole frame was shaking, his jaw and teeth chattering uncontrollably.

Standing next to the cart was an older Japanese soldier, Ben guessed he was important as the soldier with the gun saluted and lowered his weapon as the came to him.

Adachi made an assumption, the boy-man standing before him wore dirty almost ragged shorts and a patterned short sleeved shirt that had once been someone's weekend shirt. The boy was not fettered with Japanese protocol, he knew nothing of good or bad manners, he looked directly at Adachi's face. He guessed that being poor he would be Catholic and thus, maybe he spoke some English.

"Calm yourself! San Antonio! Which way?" Adachi gestured to the boy towards the diverging tracks.

Ben slowly and shakily pointed to the left one.

Takeda looked down from the cart at the still shaking boy then turned towards the Colonel.

"The boy will travel with us in this cart Colonel. Instruct him to climb on."

Colonel Adachi addressed Ben in English.

"Get in the cart and guide us."

Without looking up Ben replied.

"Sir, I cannot go without the permission of my father. He has directed me to work in this field."

Prince Takeda smiled but waited for Colonel Adachi to translate.

"Ask him where his father's house is Colonel."

'It is the hut that can be seen down the road to the right Kimsu." Adachi replied.

"Then we will go. You will take the boy Colonel and speak with his father. The boy will translate."

Esteban Valmores was asleep in a hammock when the sound of his son calling woke him. His blind eye constantly 'cried'. He wiped away the moisture as he rose and pulled down the black eyepatch.

The squat, wide, bull like Japanese colonel entered behind Ben, his presence and appearance seemed to fill all of the tin house.

"Father, the Japanese soldiers want me to guide them to San Antonio, the boss is travelling in a Carabao cart so it will take a long time. I ask your permission to go?"

"I, - I don't know, I'm not sure." He didn't say that he was worried Ben would not return, that they would simply kill him after he had guided them.

"Tell your father not to worry we will return you to him." Colonel Adachi impatiently tapped his shiny brown leather calf length gaiter with his stick. He sensed Esteban's fear. Another voice entered the room, it was Ben's uncle Limo.

"He should go to help our friends Esteban."

'Yes, Yes. You are right Limo." Esteban replied nervously wanting the important Japanese soldier to go away from his poor farmers home.

"Please look after my son."

There was no more conversation, Colonel Adachi ushered Ben out and up onto the cart.

Ben smiled at the man with a shaved head, white clothes with a red flower on them. Prince Takeda looked at Ben's shining face, shining eyes, shining teeth and smiled back.

"That way." Ben said, then sat down next to the colonel.

Somehow Prince Takeda didn't feel alone anymore.

"What is your name?" Takeda asked.

"Benhaneen. My name is Benhameen."

Prince Takeda nodded. He knew Ben didn't know what to call him, how to address him.

"It is getting late Benhameen you will show us San Antonio tomorrow. Now you will guide us to San Fernando."

"Sir I cannot, I will have to ask again for my father's permission, I will be away all night."

Ben's obedience pleased Takeda.

"Colonel Adachi, have my staff car come up, we will return to Benhameens father's house then he will guide us to San Fernando camp."

The colonel's heels clicked. He saluted and waved up the black Mercedes staff car from the rear of the convoy. The driver of the cart was dismissed.

Ben had never been in a car before.

"Colonel Adachi, tell Benhameen's father that I have decided to employ him as my valet. Inform him that he must not worry about his son's safety. I pledge to return him safely when the time comes."

Colonel Adachi was almost as wide as the doorway. Esteban Valmores had never considered his life, his home without his laughing joyful son. He lit up the darkest moments. He hung his head and accepted but did not believe the Colonel's words. he would never see his son again. Life would never be the same. Colonel Adachi turned brusquely and left the one eyed peasant to his thoughts.

San Fernando army camp was very big and ablaze with lights. The convoy slowed at the large wood framed barbed wire gates but didn't stop. The gates were quickly opened, everyone within sight bowed towards the big black Mercedes flying a white pennant flag with a red Chrysanthemum on it.

Ben whispered to Colonel Adachi.

"What does Kimsu mean?"

"Prince. It means Prince."

The convoy turned left. There were many buildings but only one house. The car stopped in front of the house. Soldiers were struggling to manoeuvre the three heavy teak slabs into a large room on the right. The driver hurried to open the door for the Prince. Takeda waved for Ben to follow. On the other side of the camp, just visible from the elevated floor of the house was another camp. A camp within a camp. Enclosed and separated by dense barbed wire fences it was illuminated and patrolled by armed guards with dogs. Inside Ben could make out thin almost naked figures, standing, squatting or lying on the ground.

The house was large and dark, built of stout timbers that acted as stilts lifting the ground floor from ground level. Large wide steps led up to the living space which was separated into rooms by paper or wooden screens. Everything in the house was free from dust and glistened with polish. Silent servants with cloth feet hovered to assist, just waiting to be summoned or dismissed. Korean women thankful for domesticity and not as comfort for soldiers. Outside was harsh and cruel, inside was soft and quiet.

Ben followed Kimsu around from room to room wondering what to do. The three teak slabs formed a large bed elevated from the floor. Women had carefully placed cushions on the bed. Prince Takeda took a pillow and positioned it lengthwise in the middle of the bed.

"You will sleep on this side Benhameen. You must never cross or touch the pillow, otherwise ------" Kimsu drew his hand across his neck. Ben understood. Kimsu smiled as he viewed the trepidation his instruction had caused his new valet.

"Tomorrow you will go with Colonel Adachi and get some new clothes from the village. I cannot have my valet looking like a poor peasant. The colonel will advise you. Now, get water and towels for me to wash. I am tired."

Ben looked over to one of the women who's eyes told him to follow her. He held the towels for Kimsu whilst he washed the dust of the day from his body. Ben had never seen a naked man before. Kimsu was the same as him.

The house woman pulled at Ben's shirt and led him into a room at the back where there was water and a cooker. There on a wooden tray was a glass jug full of water and a glass. She waved towards the bedroom.

Benhameen Valmores placed the tray on the floor by the low bed next to the sleeping prince. He looked at him, his head was shaved, he looked younger with no glasses, may be thirty, may be thirty five, he was not handsome but his face was different, although asleep he still looked as though he existed at a higher level than the rest of the world. Almost god like. He moved around the other side of the bed and lay down as close to the edge as he possibly could without falling off. As far away from the pillow as he could be. He was tired but sleep did not come for a long time.

There were three of them, all dressed in resplendent white, all had a red flower. They talked all morning, Ben supplied tea, water, cigarettes, paper, pens, everything they needed or wanted. Ben had no choice but to listen. The one who coughed all the time and had blood on his handkerchief was called Chichibu, the one who drank wine was called Asaka. Food was provided by the women but the cook was Japanese. In quiet moments Ben could see out of the window, through the hot sun and dust to the other stockade. There was always shouting and often screaming. Sometimes the sound of gunfire. Groups of the thin men would be marched off outside the camp to the hillside where there was a large cave. They just went inside, he never saw anyone come out again other than the guards. Trucks were coming everyday with new thin men for the stockade. Some trucks just went straight to the cave, they had boxes but no men. Over time the entrance to the cave became a tunnel and trucks just drove straight into it.

Kimsu became the centre of Ben's life, there was never a day off, a holiday, but that didn't matter. Once a week the black Mercedes and the lorry of soldiers would journey into the mountains. Ben would be instructed to wait with the car some thirty meters back from the entrance to a cave or tunnel. The soldiers would jump down and immediately set up two machine guns pointing towards the entrance. He was never allowed in. Kimsu and Colonel Adachi would meet with Japanese Officers, engineers, experts and specialists at the entrance then spend all day inside. When they came out a small man in his fifties would give Kimsu a rolled up waxed parchment. The parchment immediately went into a brown leather satchel that he carried. Then there would be a huge explosion as the entrance collapsed, dust would billow out and the soldiers would put away their guns. At night Ben could hear Kimsu sobbing. He never asked why but guessed it was for the mothers and wives of the thin men inside the cave. Countless slaves, prisoners of war and paid workers consigned to a blackness that would consume them all, where the king was a man with a gun and one bullet. where screams and moans could not be heard, where they had all the wealth they could ever wish for but no way to spend it. They were countless because no one wanted to count.

Ben would arise from the bed and place a small white cloth close to his hand. Wherever that was.

The next morning Kimsu would speak to the Emperor on the telephone.

Chapter 6.

"How'd you get nobbled Charlie?" The tall strong red haired Australian asked the man next to him as they were marched into the stockade.

"How did you know my name was Charlie?"

"I didn't, I call every bloke Charlie. Where you from?"

"New Mexico, most of the boys here are from there. What's your name?"

"Fred."

"How'd an Aussie get caught up in this lot?"

"Had enough of bloody sheep so took a boat to the states and enlisted, blow me if they didn't put me on a boat and send me back, well nearly back."

A Japanese guard pointed his gun and bayonet at them and screamed.

"No speak! You no speak!" Jabbing the bayonet towards them.

The stockade gates were closed on them. The Japanese guards remained outside, the marching body of ragged men stopped marching, looked around and slowly dispersed. There were no huts or anywhere to sleep, just a row of tin sheets on wooden poles that provided shelter from sun and rain, no beds, toilets, chairs, tables, nothing!

"Why do you think we're here Fred?"

"No idea but if you notice all the guys they've pulled out from the march are strong blokes. I was sixteen stone in Bataan, now I reckon I'm about twelve. a lot of the thin skinny blokes didn't make it. I reckon those Japs ain't human. They must make 'em in a factory, they certainly ain't from a woman. Why d'yu think they hate us so much Charlie.?"

Charlie and Fred crouched together in the middle of the stockade. As far away from the Japanese as they could get.

"I was talking to one of the Filipinos, those poor bastards are a lot worse off than us, they were stick thin before we started out, anyway he said that it was their bloody Emperor. They think he's a God and it's their duty to die for the Emperor, to fight and never surrender. Apparently a Japanese soldier will never surrender, it's dishonourable, they either die in battle or do themselves in. So I suppose to them we're dishonourable shit, cowards, even if we had no say in it." Charlie doodled in the sandy dirt.

"They say MacArthur and his mates got airlifted out to Australia. If you were being cynical you might say he abandoned his troops and ran away."

"Yeah! You might say that Fred. If you were cynical. You know, apparently when a Jap soldier leaves home for the army he leaves a lock of his hair and some fingernail cutting cause he expects not to come back, expects to die. Those Jap guards are cunts, one bit of shit food in four days, marching in a hundred degrees, water running into the gutters, blokes literally dying of thirst. I saw one bloke make a lunge sideways for a handful of water out of a puddle. The Jap guard just shot him in the back. He keeled over, he wasn't dead. The Jap just pushed his bayonet straight into him then kicked him off the end of his rifle. Just left him there. He was dead by then, poor sod."

"One bloke in our column was ill, he'd been shitting himself as we walked for days. There was always a gap behind him. He was pretty thin to start with. He collapsed onto the road, the Japs wouldn't allow you to help him up or anything, just keep walking. The Jap truck driver behind was laughing he deliberately steered towards him and ran him over. It was horrible, there was loud Huuuuuuu came out from the bloke then you could hear all his ribs cracking then a loud 'Pop' as his head exploded. About four other trucks went over him, just flattened him into the road. Looked like a flat dead big rabbit in the end. Made some of our lot physically sick. You walked or died, it was that simple. The bad thing is they seemed to enjoy it. As you said, they ain't human."

"Where d'yu think they were sending the rest?

"Dunno Fred but to be honest the way they were packing them into those railway trucks I was glad to get pulled out. Standing room only I would say. It was bloody hot, I reckon a fair few won't make it wherever they were going."

"I reckon they've killed thousands on this march. I reckon that's what they were told to do, kill as many as you can then we won't have to feed and water 'em. What d'yu reckon Fred?"

"Reckon you're probably right, either that or it was the disgust they felt for us. The officers on the horses were worst, just galloping through, swinging and chopping. I saw one group laughing and practicing beheading blokes, apparently it's good if you can do it in one clean swing and not hack away at a blokes neck. Sends shivers down me spine just thinking about it. Don't think I'll ever forget that sight."

"Yeah, know what you mean. Before we started out I was with this group of fellas, they took us into a field and took everything off us, money, rings, photo's, letters, everything. There was this captain and two other blokes who had some Jap money on them. They took all three of 'em behind a stand of bamboo and shot em, there and then. Presume they thought they'd taken it off dead Jap soldiers. After that all the blokes on the road got rid of anything Jap pretty quick. D'yu think they'll give us some grub here Charlie?"

"Well let's think it through, if we assume we've been pulled out because we look physically OK then in all probability they will be making us work somewhere. So! If that's the case I would think yes, they'll have to feed us."

"Some of the blokes are crowding around over there, what d'yu think it is?"

"Look the grounds wet. My guess is it's a tap, let's go."

Chapter 7.

KImsu never dined with any of the generals. He always dined alone unless there was another prince visiting. Then there was wine. Tonight he had dined alone as usual. The Korean woman served the fish dish the Japanese cook had prepared. After dinner he smoked and studied the waxed parchment maps he kept in his satchel or wrote letters to his family.

Ben busied himself preparing Kimsu's white tunic for tomorrow, cleaning his shoes and preparing his bathroom ready for his nighttime bath.

It was ten thirty. Ben dropped the mosquito nets around the bed and placed a glass of water on the floor beside the bed. There had been no explosions today so there was no need for the white hankie.

At eleven Kimsu came into the bedroom and lay down. Ben waited til he was settled than turned out the lights and lay on the other side of the pillow. Ben never spoke except when Kimsu wanted to talk.

It was as though the wooden room protected them. The massive thick heavy teak slabs that formed the bed were immoveable. The beautiful lamps, bowls, vases, and ornaments just existed on the wood floor and paneling as though they had been painted there. The Korean woman polished everything with beeswax. The wood seemed thankful for it, breathing in and out with the wind, the light and the dark. Although the compound was near enough for Ben to hear the moans, the screams and occasional gunshot, somehow the wooden house made it not real, made it go away.

"Benhameen, are you awake?"

"Yes Kimsu."

"Do you know why we are here Benhameen?"

"I know why I am here Kimsu. I am your servant and I am very happy to be the servant of a great leader."

"No Ben, I mean do you know why I, the Japanese are here?"

"Yes Kimsu, the Japanese are here to help us escape from colonialism."

Prince Takeda let out a sad sigh. Quietly he spoke.

"No Benhameen, we are here to conquer and control countries and people, to use them, to kill them and steal all their gold."

"Why would you do that Kimsu?"

"Because my Emperor wants it. The red flower you see on my tunic is a Chrysanthemum flower, the throne of Japan is called the 'Chrysanthemum Throne'. The people think the Emperor is a god. His words cannot be questioned, his slightest wish is a command that must be obeyed. His flower has sixteen petals, the flower of a prince, my flower, has only fourteen."

"Is he a god Kimsu?"

"No he is a man, just like you and I Benhameen, but not as beautiful as you." Prince Takeda chuckled.

"Why does he want everybody's gold Kimsu?"

"So that the Chrysanthemum Throne can become the richest throne in the world. Japan can be the richest country in the world. Then he can control the world and the world must live as he directs. --------------In peace."

"That is good Kimsu."

"No, it's not good Benhameen, people don't want to give us their gold, their silver, their diamonds, so we have to take it. To take it we kill thousands and thousands of people Benhameen. Thousands of people. It is me they look to, to blow up a cave entrance. In the cave is the gold and diamonds we have taken from people. The good people who have worked to extend and prepare the cave. I kill, no one must know the secrets of the cave so the soldiers force them deep inside then I kill them with darkness. The soldiers as well."

"Are you happy Kimsu. You are very rich."

"No Benhameen, I am not happy, I am a prisoner, just as much as the men in the stockade. There are thousands of souls screaming at me, outside of the stockade. The gates are open but I dare not go out. Goodnight Benhameen."

"Goodnight Kimsu."

"Ben."

"Yes Kimsu."

"You must never speak of our conversations. They are private. Between friends."

"Yes Kimsu."

Chapter 8.

"Told you they'd feed us, there's a cart with what looks like rice and soup coming towards us and everyone's moving over towards the gates."

"You could be right Fred, let's go."

There were about two hundred men in the stockade, more would come everyday but everyday two or three lorry loads would leave. No one ever came back.

Guards with sticks and guns forced everyone into a long queue. Women dished out the rice onto banana leaves, another woman gave out dried fish then at the end of the tables was a large drum of hot watery vegetable broth. It wasn't a soup. It was lukewarm. Men dipped in a mug which was attached by wire to the drum and drank it there and then. It was an old metal oil drum.

As they queued a Japanese Officer walked along the line looking at them. Every now and again he'd stop and stamp a mark in red ink onto the back of the right hand.

"Don't look at him Charlie. Don't know what it is but I feel uncomfortable about it."

"Me too Fred."

Fred and Charlie stared at the ground as they shuffled forward. The officer closed in on them. Both Fred and Charlie were stamped.

The rice was not good but there was enough of it. The fish was tough, full of bones but tasty, the broth, more of a flavoured drink than a broth. It was the best and most food they'd eaten since they'd been marched away from Bataan.

"Which suite do you want Fred, the 'penthouse' or the 'honeymoon'?"

"Well we're not married yet Charlie so I'm for the four poster and silk sheets in the 'penthouse'."

As night came and the flood lights came on both men lay down in the dust and dirt of the stockade. All the spaces under the tin roofs had long since been taken. The night shift of mosquitos flitted silently and hungrily from skin to skin. Sawing their way without pain through the skin to the succulent blood vessel.

"What d'yu reckon this red stamp's about Charlie?"

"Dunno Fred, 'spect we'll find out in the morning."

The morning sun brought no food but did bring guards who pulled out all the men with red stamps and herded them together just to the right of the gate. Altogether there were about fifty blokes, all wearing just shorts. About ten armed guards stood around them with fingers on the triggers of their rifles. Other guards called up prisoners one at a time and fitted ankle chains. The chains were heavy, the manacles were thick and heavy, they caused pain and injury to the men but the guards didn't care. Three trucks lined up outside the gate.

"Looks as though we're off on a mystery tour Fred."

"Hope they stop at a pub. I could sink a beer or two."

"Come on Fred, you know beer's bad for your health."

"No Charlie. Japs are bad for your health!"

The humour was spoken but no one laughed.

It was difficult climbing up onto the high truck wearing ankle chains. Some of the prisoners helped to lift up one chap then he helped pull up the next chap and so on. The Jap guards counted on twenty to a truck then three armed guards got in the back as well. Two other armed guards got in the front with the driver. The morning sun was getting strong and hot as the trucks drove off.

Nobody spoke much on the truck. It was a bumpy road and the driver liked to accelerate as quick as possible then brake as hard as possible. Everyone held onto the side of the truck or someone else. Soldiers holding hands was OK. The trucks had been going for about two hours, the outskirts of Manila presented what appeared to be normal life, people walking, talking, shopping, sitting drinking coffee, hanging out washing, trees, gardens, motorbikes,cars, children playing. Japanese soldiers and military vehicles were everywhere.

"This looks a bit Spanish Charlie, looks quite old."

"Where d'yu think we are Fred?"

"Dunno but a while back I saw a sign saying 'BanBang', funny names in the Philippines ain't they? Like their 'A's."

The trucks slowed to enter an ornate brick gate topped with a carved frieze. The narrow road was lined with cypress trees and on the right was a curved stone gallery with enamelled pictures and marble plaques.

"It's a bloody cemetery Fred, they've brought us to a bloody cemetery. That's not a good sign is it?"

"Well I have visited more cheerful places Charlie. I have to admit it."

The trucks stopped in front of what appeared to be the main chapel or building. It looked like a building site. Huge piles of sand, mounds of bagged cement, steel, wood, machines, vehicles. The site was massive. Literally hundreds of men were shovelling, mixing, carrying, moving everything in through the large wide carved wood doors. It was like a large open mouth that was swallowing everything. Armed Japanese soldiers were everywhere. There was no talking. just shouted instructions and obvious violence as workers were hit with sticks, hit with rifles, hit with rope, hit with wire to make them work harder, faster. Two bunkers of machine guns were posted about fifty meters away from the entrance aimed at the doors

"Look at that Fred. You wouldn't treat an animal like that would you?"

Charlie muttered as the Japanese guards shouted them down from the truck.

The men working outside made no attempt to look or communicate with them.

"These blokes look very thin Fred. Grub can't be up to much."

A Japanese guard screamed at Charlie and slammed the butt of his rifle into Charlie's right shoulder

"No speak. You no speak."

Charlie staggered forward but didn't fall. The heavy metal ankle clamp immediately produced blood as Charlie lunged forward trying to stay upright. Fred moved to help him but the forbidding glare of the guard stopped him.

All the men were now down from the truck. The guards pushed them towards the dark entrance.

Inside was a large crypt. Either side were banks of the ancient dead, fading photos, dust filled inscriptions fronted every curved tomb front. This was where the rich Catholic elite of Manila came to find their God.

"Cheerful little place." Fred half whispered, half hissed without moving his lips.

It was large, about fifty meters long. Power cables and the paraphernalia of major construction ran the length of it until finally disappearing down a flight of grey marble steps. The group of twenty men were being moved towards the steps. The only sound was the rattling of their leg manacles on the marble floor. Whispering without moving your mouth or lips when the guards weren't looking was the only safe way to communicate.

At the bottom of the stairs was another large crypt. The stone sides the same as above but stained with seeping water and age. It smelt of damp, of old air, as though the occupants were simply waiting. It didn't smell of death. The lines ran the length of it then down another flight of stairs.

"What d'yu think the Japs are doing here Fred?" Charlie hissed.

"No idea, may be they're extending it for all the dead Japs that have been killed here. Expect there were loads when they invaded." Fred and Charlie were in the middle of the shuffling group. Their whispers were inaudible above the scraping chains. The group descended the steps to another large crypt but this time there were no stairs at the end of it. At the end, going straight ahead, to the right and to the left were large concrete lined tunnels. At the end of them thin sweating men were hacking away making the tunnels longer. Japanese engineers were stood around with clipboards or plans directing steel, concrete, shuttering, mixing. Japanese guards stood and watched. If a worker stopped working he was beaten, if he fell he was shot. To fall was to die.

"It's the same as the bloody march here Fred." Charlie whispered.

A tall white man with protruding ribs and diarrhoea running out of his tattered shorts fell to his knees in front of the earth wall. A guard glanced towards an officer who nodded. In an instant the bayonet was through his thin frame, the point protruding from his chest. There was just a prolonged gurgle as he fell forward. It was over for him. Nobody moved to pick him up or remove his body until the guard instructed them. Worked to death came to Fred's mind.

The ankle chains were replaced with guns that pointed at you. Fred and Charlie worked eighteen hour days along with hundreds of others. Rice, and vegetable flavoured water just about kept them alive, somedays they'd get some rotten fish. Never any meat. Time disappeared, not knowing what day it was, what month it was, what year it was didn't matter as the sun or moon was never seen. An electric bulb was the sun. Darkness was the moon. Home was a concrete floor. The toilet was a banana leaf or a steel drum.

Some sought an end to it, kneeling down with a bowed head waiting for a sword or a bayonet. They'd stopped shooting them because of the noise. The Japs always did it in full view of everybody as a frightening lesson.

In the dark, before sleep took them away from it they talked in whispers.

"D'yu think your brain still thinks when they've chopped your head off Charlie?"

"Dunno, suppose it must do for a few seconds."

"What about your eyes? D'yu think you still see?"

"Suppose you must do. Your eyes are very close to your brain, so until your brain packs up you must be able to see."

"How long d'yu think it takes for your brain to pack up?"

"No idea but the other day when they did that bald headed bloke in I'm sure he looked at me after his head had rolled onto the floor. Never forget it. Horrible it was."

"How long d'yu think we've been here Fred?"

"No idea, a long long time Charlie, I know that. We've been working in this cavern for ages and there was two before. Mind you, this one's the biggest."

"Apparently they've been driving lorries into the other two and stacking them floor to ceiling with big heavy boxes, takes about four to six men to lift one box. What d'yu think's in them?"

"The only thing I can think of that's heavy is gold. There's lead of course but they ain't gonna build massive vaults like this for lead. I reckon they're building up a nest egg in case the war goes wrong. What do you think Fred?"

There was no reply Fred was deep in sleep on the dry dusty concrete floor. They'd both wore the same pair of shorts since they entered. They stank but so did everything so it didn't matter.

Chapter 9.

The army camp at San Fernando had been Ben's home for over two years. His life was luxurious heaven compared to the slaves and prisoners, even to some of the Japanese soldiers. He shared the company of Generals who protected him from bad things because he was 'Kimsu's boy'. Shared the best food, travelled in a big car. Slept on a bed. Kimsu's bed.

Once or twice a week they'd go out to visit a site. Kimsu usually visited a site three times. Once to look at a cave, a hole in the ground, a mineshaft, an air vent shaft, an underground basement or vault and say whether or not it was suitable for development. Once to view it when the work was finished or very nearly finished and finally a visit to record an inventory of what was in there. The last visit was usually just Kimsu and a general. It was the nights after a last visit that Ben left a white hankie with his water. The engineers would assemble outside waiting to move on to the next site. The slaves and prisoners never came out. Kimsu would spend a long time praying in his 'dark' room on those nights. There were many such nights.

One special night there had been a dinner at the house. Takeda, Prince Chichibu, Prince Asaka, Prince Makasa and Prince Takamatsu. There was wine and special food. That day they had all visited Matsushiro, a very large bunker complex near Nagano. It was so big it was almost an underground town. Ten thousand Korean slaves had built it. They never came out. The Japanese soldiers manning the machine gun posts never came out. The explosions were very big and powerful. Enough to shake a mountain. Now the wine was helping them to forget, helping to swill away the dust of death. Songs provided a space for time to fill as though it wasn't part of their doing. Not part of their world.

Ben 'hovered' in the shadows in the corner of the large room. He didn't serve food, he wasn't a waiter but he liked to be there in case Kimsu needed him.

Prince Takeda was at ease in the company of his peers. He put down the wine glass and looked around for Ben. Spotting him in the corner of the room he waved him over.

He spoke in English.

"Benhameen, we've run out of salt, go into the tunnels at the back of the camp take the left tunnel and then the first tunnel on the right. There you will find some blue steel drums. One of them is full of salt, take a large bowl, fill it up and bring it back. Do you understand?"

"Yes Kimsu. What about the guards?"

"They know who you are Benhameen, just take the bowl and tell them your task." Prince Takeda turned away to resume his conversation with Prince Asaka.

Ben moved from the light of the house, through the darkness to the lights of the camp and the tunnels behind it. He had a large green and white porcelain bowl. It was exquisitely decorated Celadon porcelain stolen from Korea. He showed it to the guards.

"Salt for Prince Takeda."

The guards waved him through. It took him five minutes of walking to reach the right hand tunnel. It was stacked high with wooden boxes, below them were the blue steel drums, they had lids on them but were not fastened. He looked into the first drum and saw it was two thirds full of gemstones, all sorts, red ones, green ones, blue ones and white ones he thought might be diamonds. Putting his hand in he let the glittering hard stones rattle through his fingers. He wondered where they had come from, what stories they could tell, how much love was in them.

Ben put the lid back loosely on top and looked in the next drum. It was nearly full of gold coins, all shapes and sizes but all gold in colour. He forced his hand in but it was difficult as the coins were heavy he lifted out three or four in the palm of his hand and looked at them. Suddenly there was a metallic click behind him. Dropping the coins back into the drum Ben turned to see a guard aiming his rifle at him. The guard started shouting for other guards to come over. Within seconds there were two more. Ben held up the bowl. He was shaking and scared.

"Salt! Salt for Prince Takeda." Ben spoke in English hoping that one of them would understand. Two of the guards levelled their rifles at him and clicked off the safety catches. One guard came over and took the bowl from him before searching his clothes and him. He found nothing and waved down the weapons. He pointed to the end drum. Ben picked up the bowl and lifted the lid on the end drum. It was full of salt.

The guards escorted Ben and the bowl of salt to the house and reported their story to a Japanese attendant who conveyed it to Prince Takeda. There was much laughter. The guards were dismissed.

The drinking and laughter carried on into the early hours of the next day. The wine would replace the hanky tonight. Ben waited in the bedroom waiting for Kimsu to finish his prayers. They both fell asleep quickly in the silent dark room.

The next morning Ben could not move. Dare not move. Surrounding him on the hard dark teak slab were gold coins in small stacks two or three high. The coins had been carefully positioned to form a continuous line around his body.

"Kimsu." Ben called out softly as his Prince was asleep.

"Kimsu, please Kimsu, help me."

Prince Takeda supported himself on one elbow and laughed over the pillow that divided them. He called out loudly, the other princes slowly came into the room to laugh at a trembling but immoveable Ben.

"Kimsu, please help me." He repeated.

"Get up Ben, it's just a joke from last night, collect up the coins, give them to your father when you see him as payment for taking his son away."

Ben got up feeling uncomfortable at being seen in Prince Takeda's bed. It meant nothing to the royal visitors.

Chapter 10.

"What's going on Charlie? Listen I can hear singing."

"Dunno Fred but something's happening I can hear a lot of shouting. The Japs are shouting 'Banzai'."

The site at BanBang underground cemetery was huge, tunnels big enough for two lorries to pass, three chambers, two of which were the size of football pitches, the height of two houses. Thousands and thousands of slaves and prisoners were living and dying there. For months now lorries had been arriving daily. Their golden cargo unloaded and carefully stacked high. Food was trolleyed in, in steel oil drums. Shit and piss was trolleyed out in steel oil drums.

It was a celebration. It was the last and largest site to be completed. The last of one hundred and seventy two sites that peppered the mountains and islands of the Philippines. The site was finished. All the maps were in Prince Takeda's leather satchel. Stolen gold and silver was stacked high, drums of gemstones, gold coins, silver jewellery, bank notes and anything precious lined the walls.

Princes Takeda and Chichibu, Generals Yamashita and Adachi were there to congratulate the engineers, the electricians, the experts in every field, even the Japanese Army lorry drivers and guards had been invited. Wine flowed and the food was good. The banquet was deep inside the maze of tunnels. Ben had been instructed by Kimsu to lay a red chord from the entrance to the banquet as they walked in, just in case they got drunk and couldn't remember the way out. It was a very long thin chord.

Handshakes, laughter, singing, smiles and shouts of 'Banzai' were ubiquitous and echoed along and through the tunnels. Prince Takeda sat next to his family friend Navy Captain Honda who had been heroic in managing the vast site. It was late, the exhausted stick thin workers heard it, ignored it and slept on. Sleep and rest were commodities not to be wasted by 'wondering'.

General Yamashita was a hero of the Japanese people. His unstoppable sweep from French Indo China towards Malaya and Singapore had taken only seventy days and although outnumbered his troops had taken eighty thousand prisoners of war when Singapore capitulated. Now the war was not going well. General MacArthur was seeking revenge and about to invade the Philippines. Yamashita had been drafted in at the last moment to save them. To work his magic again. The Emperor had been convinced that the Philippines would always belong to Japan whatever the outcome of the war, he had ordered the hiding of the stolen war gold in the islands but now things had changed. With MacArthur everything was personal.

It was twelve midnight, glances were exchanged. Princes and Generals quietly slipped away.

"I insist the boy remains Your Highness." Despite the wine General Yamashita was formal. His military decorations that littered his uniform just supported his round long moustached face. His formality stopped at the red flower on the white tunic.

"The boy is my valet. He comes with me General."

General Yamashita moved closer to Prince Takeda.

"Sir. I must insist. This boy knows everything, he's been to all the sites with you, been inside some sites including this one. Knows what is in them. You will be jeopardizing the Emperor's plans for Japan if you bring this boy out. He's a Philippino farm boy, he has no allegiance, no loyalty to the throne. He is a danger to our country's future". Yamashita's hissed but quiet delivery and fierce glare were directed at Prince Takeda's throat. He dared not go higher.

"His allegiance and loyalty lie with me General. I made a promise to his father that I would return him safely. A prince of the Chrysanthemum Throne does not fail to honour a promise."

"I've heard that Prince Takeda. That the boy does lie with you." General Yamashita turned and almost marched away following the red chord. Prince Takeda, his valet and Prince Chichibu followed.

Outside the entrance Prince Takeda nodded to the soldier and seconds later the earth shook.

The small convoy headed back towards San Fernando camp. There were two staff cars, Princes Takeda, Chichibu and Ben followed by Generals Yamashita and Adachi. There was no conversation. Takeda was sobbing into a white hanky Ben passed to him. Chichibu was coughing blood into his own hanky.

First of all everything shook, then the lights went out, seconds later came a blasted rushing cloud of hot dust that covered everything, choked everything. Then the awful silent still blackness.

"Fred! Fred! What the fuck has happened. Fred! Are you OK?"

Fred cleared his throat. The blackness was total.

"No idea Charlie. It sounded like, felt like a huge explosion."

"May be the Yanks have invaded. I heard a new bloke talking about it. There's thousands of us in here so they must have to dig us out if it's blocked. What do we do now Charlie?"

"I don't know Fred. I don't know what to do. I can't see a thing, it's like being blind. Listen other blokes are shouting and talking."

The hum of quiet talking gradually got louder as realization and panic started to increase with the temperature. There was no light, no air, no electricity., nothing but the darkness.

In the tunnels time was only measured by eating, drinking, sleeping, going to the toilet and working. There was nothing else. Electric light brought about an eternal day. The Japanese guards punished talking or resting, now they were shouting but there was no one to hear them. Now there was eternal night. Now there was no way to measure time. A watch just went round in the darkness. It meant nothing.

"I think this is it Fred. The end of the line."

"No It can't be, there's loads of Jap guards, lorry drivers, blokes at the machine guns, they ain't gonna give up on their own are they? No it's some sort of accident or a bombing. No, the Japs will be frantically organizing stuff to open it up. They're hardly likely to abandon all this gold are they?"

"Can't do anything about it Fred, just lie here I suppose. If the air runs out before they get to us we're gonnas."

"Don't think like that Charlie, just lie still and stay calm."

"OK, getting hot in here ain't it."

Chapter 11.

Royal Prince Tsunehisa Takeda had lived with Filipino farm boy Benhameen Valmores since June 1942. It was now late 1944 and the Americans were closing in. General Douglas MacArthur was out for revenge having been forced to flee, leaving thousands of his men to the mercy of the Japanese. Japan didn't have much mercy.

Kimsu and Ben had never touched. They had slept on the same bed every night for over two years, separated by a pillow. Takeda liked the comfort of closeness, the sounds of life, someone to talk to in quiet times. When they were alone they spoke in English. Ben had been taught English by Father Disney at the Catholic School. In the day time, in public, Takeda always spoke to Ben in Japanese to be translated by someone. He had warned Ben that if they ever touched over the pillow he would have to kill him for he was the cousin of a living god. Everynight Ben prayed that his sleep would not move him near the pillow.

Prince Takeda commanded thousands. Soldiers, officers, miners, engineers, electricians, cartographers, architects, ceramics experts, explosives experts, prisoners of war and just plain slaves. None dared to look above the red and gold chrysanthemum on the left breast of the white tunic. Ben knew nothing of Japan, of the war, of the Chrysanthemum Throne or its deadly instructions that could never be questioned. He saw the absolute reverence that slaves and Generals gave to Kimsu but Ben loved and served him as a father, with laughter in his eyes, truth in his voice and cheerful love that flowed out like waves.

Takeda was lonely. A long way from his home and family. For two years Ben had done everything for him. Laundered his clothes, presented his food, fetched his wine, his cigarettes, his water but most of all he looked into his face and eyes with a smile that lit up the room. Lit up his dreadful life. Made what he was doing go away. And now it was time for him to go away. Back to a defeated country on the verge of surrender. A country immensely and secretly rich. Where the poor had died in their millions without knowing the real reason why.

Kimsu called Ben into the small back room of the house in San Fernando. The room was dark. A shrine with ceremonial swords, daggers, hangings and a large wooden altar bearing a painted back panel of the ancient Buddhist monk Nichiren. There was no photo, no painting of his uncle The

Emperor Hirohito. It was not permitted. Japan had never heard the Emperor's voice.

Takeda had had the walls lined with dark wood panels, the floor was teak and the ceiling diamond shaped wood panels. It always smelt fragrant from burning incense. He had made it his church, his special place, after his tears he would come here. Ben had never been in it, he had seen inside it when Kimsu entered or left. A Korean woman who was a slave in the San Fernando Army camp came and cleaned it every day.

Ben followed Kimsu into the small room, on the floor was a soiled Japanese battle flag, the sort that fluttered from the top of a tank radio aerial. For the first time Kimsu touched Ben as he held the top of his arms and directed him to stand opposite him over the flag.

Ben was the same height as Kimsu, he looked for explanation on the Prince's face, from his eyes but Kimsu's face was lowered, looking at the flag and chanting 'Asha Asha Asha'-- . Ben counted ten times. Kimsu raised his head and looked into Ben's eyes as he drew out a shining steel dagger from the sheath on his red belt. Was this it? Was this the time of his death? Of their death? Was this how he was going to die? Would it hurt? He would die for Kimsu. He would die now.

"Asha Asha Asha" Kimsu began chanting again. He transferred the dagger to his left hand and raised his right hand. In an instant he sliced the finger tip off the little finger of his right hand. Blood flowed and dripped onto the flag. Slowly he moved the dagger back to his bloody right hand. All the time chanting 'Asha Asha Asha', then taking Ben's right hand grasped the little finger and sliced. Prince Takeda had not winced at the pain, he knew it was coming, Ben gasped and dragged away his bleeding hand but his blood still spilt onto the flag.

"We are now as brothers Benahmeen." Kimsu looked directly into Ben's wet almost crying eyes.

"As father and son, as son and father, as family. You can now touch me and I wouldn't have to kill you. Tonight I must leave for Japan. Probably I will never see you again. I thank you for your service to me and the other Princes. I cannot take you with me. You must never reveal or talk about me or Prince Chichibu or any of the other princes you have served, never reveal our names. Never tell anyone about the locations we have closed. Now I must return you to your father as I promised."

Ben had slipped to his knees and was now crying. The blood from his finger was now dripping slowly onto the flag. The physical hurt was over, nothing more than a sting. Ben had never thought about the future, only knew about soldiers and not the war. Hadn't thought about life without Kimsu. He was a Prince. He could do anything, have anything, fix anything.

"Get up Ben, go wash your hand and bandage your finger then get the guard outside to summon my car." As always, Ben obeyed. Kimsu rolled up the flag and put it in his leather satchel where he kept his maps.

Kimsu's car was a big long open topped black Mercedes. The folding fabric roof was usually neatly layered onto the rear valance. It was always accompanied by an open truck with at least ten, sometimes fifteen heavily armed soldiers. There were no seats in the back of the truck, just high steel sides topped by steel mesh. This time there were twelve soldiers and six almost naked Korean slaves. As Kimsu emerged from the house the driver sprang out to open the door, bowing and staring at the floor as the prince and his valet climbed in and sat down. Ben had dressed Prince Takeda in a clean white tunic as a few spots of blood had splashed onto the legs of his first tunic. Kimsu had not bandaged his hand, it was now just a clump of dark red congealed blood on the end of his finger. Ben had summoned the cleaning lady to bandage his finger but the blood had seeped through. It had been difficult to dress Kimsu without getting more blood on the new tunic but he had done it. Normally he would have worn gloves so as not to touch Prince Takeda but now, today, he didn't. Things had changed.

It was dusk, nearly dark, evenfall, as the small convoy moved slowly out of San Fernando Army Camp. The small pennant flag on the front of the Mercedes made everyone bow, their eyes locked safely onto the ground as it passed by. The wet jungle either side of the road was alive with night noise as crickets celebrated the recent shower of rain. No one spoke but as they travelled Ben saw they were heading towards his home village. His father's home.

Ben could feel Kimsu's body next to him. Every time the car jolted their shoulders touched. He wondered what life would be like without his beloved prince to serve, to fetch water for, to look at, to hear sobbing at night when on his order hundreds of men and women were machine gunned to death in a tunnel they had laboured to build or had simply been shut in a blackness that would eventually suffocate them. He knew no one who smoked a cigarette like Kimsu, between his forefinger and his little finger. Would that change now the end of his little finger had gone?

Now they were at his father's house. Esteban came out to greet them. Smiling when he saw his son was safe and well. The soldiers had pushed the shackled slaves out of the truck throwing some shovels onto the ground behind them then instructing them to lug two heavy bronze boxes towards the house, before driving off to park five hundred meters away out of sight behind some bamboo thickets.

Ben's family house was small but it sat in a large plot. Water was collected from rain as it bounced and ran off the corrugated steel roof. The land behind was separated into areas for pigs and chickens, vegetable plots and a small flower garden. At the very back, fed by a small stream were fruit trees growing happily in a large bare earth circle of land that the pigs and chickens fought over in the day time.

Esteban acknowledged Kimsu with a small bow and hugged his son with a large smile. Despite assurances Esteban hadn't really expected to see his son again. Talk of the Japanese Army had been dreadful within the small village. Everyone knew someone who had been taken as a worker or slave to dig tunnels.

There was no interpreter but no other Japanese present. Kimsu spoke to Ben in English.

"Ask your father to select a spot at the rear of his garden where we can bury these boxes."

Esteban, Ben and Kimsu followed the light of a torch to a sandy spot between a mango tree and a banyan tree. Kimsu called the slaves over and marked out a rectangle with a stick in the bare sand.

It took them an hour to dig a large pit two meters deep. A soldier with a rifle stood guard at the house fifty meters away. The slaves were visibly relieved when they were instructed to drag over the two boxes and lower them into the pit. Their fear had been palpable that they were digging their own graves.

The last slave in the pit was instructed to open up the boxes. Inside were chunks of gold. Seventy five kilo gold bars had been sawn up into small pieces. It didn't look anything, chunks of dirty almost brown metal that just filled the boxes. Kimsu handed down a small tin of powder with instructions to sprinkle it over the gold then close the boxes. The last slave came out the pit. It took them twenty minutes of shovelling to fill it in. The beads of sweat on their backs attracted night time mosquitoes that gorged on blood then moved an inch to gorge some more. Their irritating bite came a poor second to fear.

Kimsu lifted his bloodied right hand towards the guard. The guard called up the slaves and marched them over to the truck.

"This is for you Benahmeen, when the Americans have gone dig it up, sell some, buy a big ranch, marry a pretty girl and have lots of children."

Ben's father was nearby, so he couldn't show the emotion he felt.

"Please take me with you Kimsu. I will serve you faithfully for the rest of my life."

Prince Takeda ignored his plea. It was impossible. He lived in a different world. One where heredity and birth were everything and love meant nothing.

"When you open a box Benhameen, pour gasoline over it and burn it. That will remove the poison."

He ignored Ben's quiet tugging at the sleeve of his tunic. The heat of the night was closing in, insects were attracted to his wounded finger. It was time to go.

A fusillade of crackling gunfire silenced the night sounds. It was close by, Ben could hear bullets zipping into thin naked bodies, almost hear the smashing of bones. There was some screaming but not much, more a grunting, a gasping, then it was silent. Then the engine of the lorry started up and got fainter as it drove away.

He could see tears in Kimsu's eyes. For all the death, for the thousands his orders had killed, every time he felt it, be it one or a hundred in a tunnel, the fault, the blame came down on him just as heavily. The load got no lighter with numbers. It was for the Emperor, not for mothers.

It was the first time Ben had been with Kimsu in the car without an armed escort of soldiers. Times were changing. Japan was losing the war. The Americans were coming. Life would not be the same.

The driver was small and the steering wheel of the Mercedes was white and big. The car headed north towards Aparri. Kimsu and Ben sat in silence as it carefully travelled the road, the yellow light from the big lights scattering the nighttime population of the road. Ben could see that Kimsu's wounded hand was now giving him pain. The Korean woman who had dressed Ben's hand had given him a few tablets that helped to quell his pain. Ben passed them to Kimsu.

After two hours they entered the town and drove slowly towards the docks. By now it was late, nearly midnight. Tied up at the small jetty was a black submarine. Ben had never seen a submarine before and didn't really know what it was. Kimsu saw the bewilderment on his face.

Kimsu smiled.

"It's a ship that travels under the water Benhameen. The Americans have many ships between here and Japan so my family have sent this submarine to take me home."

Prince Takeda climbed out of the Mercedes. The driver looked guilty that he hadn't had time to open the door.

"Goodbye Benhameen, remember never tell anyone about me or any of the other princes you have come to know."

Ben half nodded half bowed and handed Kimsu the brown leather satchel. As he raised his head their eyes met. Both were moist with heavy emotion, both looked deep into what could have been.

Kimsu started chanting Asha Asha Asha and turned to go.

"Wait here Ben, do not go yet."

He turned and walked along the small thin plank and onto the vessel. The gang plank was lined with bowing sailors.

The driver of the Mercedes was silent, motionless behind the wheel. looking straight ahead. It was better not to see but he couldn't shut out the quiet conversation that was so heavy with emotion and sorrow that it caused a million questions.

After about ten minutes Prince Takeda returned. He was dressed in simple western clothes, brown trousers and a short sleeved shirt. He handed his white tunic, sword and dagger to Ben.

"Remember your promise to me Ben, never tell anyone, Americans, Japanese, Philippino's. No one. Tell no one about what you have seen, what you know, or where places are. Tell no one about me or any of the Princes who have been here. Tell no one their names. Asha! Asha! Asha!"

Ben reached out and held his Prince's right hand lifting it up to bring the congealed mess closer.

"Kimsu you must get your finger dressed on the boat. It will go bad and you will die. If I hear that has happened I will not want to live."

Ben was not looking at Takeda's hand he was looking deep into his eyes but felt the warmth of it.

The sailors lining the gangplank were all stood to attention. As soon as Prince Takeda turned away from Ben towards the plank they dropped their head and eyes to the ground.

The wind coming across the bay was increasing. The small submarine rocked restlessly on its lines. The sailors' collars blew up behind their necks and hats. It was as though it blew a message to the sad Prince that it was time to go. The captain uneasy when not protected by the deep sea.

Prince Takeda mounted the gang plank with no backward glance towards the beautiful youth who had been his servant and companion for the last two and half years.

Ben got back in the rear of the Mercedes, he wondered if he should have got in the front. The driver started the engine and engaged a gear.

"No." Ben drew an imaginary line with his hand. The driver turned off the engine. Ben pointed to his eyes and then made a wave motion with his hands. The driver understood that Ben wanted to wait until the black low ship had left.

The sailors had just started to ship the gangplank when Prince Takeda reappeared on deck. He ordered the sailors to push out the plank then within seconds he was back with Ben.

"Benhameen take my satchel. It has all the maps for all the 'Golden Lily' sites." He paused. "The graves of many men. Take it, bury it in a box, tell no one about it. If I have not come back for it within thirty years take it to my family. Remember Benhameen, tell no one, The Police, The Army, The Government, The Americans, The Japanese, The Filipinos. No one. I give it to you in case the submarine doesn't make it. "

Ben clasped the satchel to his chest and his prince was gone.

It was an almost silent departure, the slap of the waves changed slightly as the submarine inched away from the dark jetty, its diesels coughing out dirty fumes into the night air, matching black with black. Within minutes it had disappeared.

Estaban immediately hid as he heard the sound of an engine arrive and stop at the front of his tin home. The thirty seconds of crackling spitting death he had heard a few hours ago made him petrified. Were the soldiers coming back for the boxes. Were they going to kill him! Then he heard the voice of his beloved son.

"Papa! Papa! Where are you?" Esteban emerged noisily from under a pile of rusty corrugated sheets at the back of the house and hugged his son.

"You are safely home Benahmeen! Tomorrow we will kill a pig and celebrate."

Ben went into the small lean-to at the side of the house. It was as it was two and a half years ago except his bedding had been washed and folded up neatly on the end of his mattress. The mosquito net was tied up with ribbon and the few clothes he had were washed, ironed and folded in his small cupboard that had no doors.

Ben sat down on his bed and looked at the sword, drawing it out of the scabbard. It was a dark almost black metal, very sharp and very hard. Unlike any other metal he'd ever seen. It would be good for cutting cane or bamboo. He stroked and felt Kimsu's white tunic. The red and gold flower was so dominant, so fascinating. It was all people looked at, the white tunic merely served as a regal background to the flower. It caused all people to bow, lower themselves to the ground or hide. He would bury the satchel tomorrow. Now he would sleep.

Early the next morning Ben put the satchel in an old suitcase and buried it between the stream that fed the fruit trees and the pig's hut. He buried it deep so the pigs wouldn't dig it up and eat it. It took a while.

The small black submarine lowered itself into the safety of the depths. Prince Takeda accustomed himself to the smells and creaks of the vessel as it started out on the three thousand kilometre dark journey. They would travel the rest of the night and all of the next day under the sea. He couldn't stop himself thinking about the thousands of people he had condemned to a dark hot airless end. If his life ended in a dark wet crushed tube at the bottom of the deep ocean, it would be fair. A Medic with a bowed head suggested he cleaned and dressed his finger. It made him think of Ben and the love he'd left behind. The Captain offered him his bunk. Prince Takeda lay on it. Eventually sleep came.

Chapter 12.

"You have done well Prince Takeda, the treasure you have hidden in the Philippines makes the Chrysanthemum Throne the richest house in the world. Soon we will introduce the teachings of Nichiren to that world. I am sad that our people have had to die but their descendants will come to understand why."

Emperor Hirohito and Prince Takeda sat at an elegant French table in the corner of the large library room. Ancient manuscripts, text and books from all over occupied Southeast Asia and China filled the shelves. The more valuable ones were in glass cases. There was no dust in the room.

The Emperor was always formal, it was eleven in the morning. His morning suit simply complemented his moustache and gold glasses. His cousin, Prince Takeda wore his white tunic. The red flower was the only embellishment.

"But the war is being lost Your Excellency. Tojo tells me that the Americans are firebombing many of our towns and cities."

"The war is of no consequence Takeda. We now have the means to control and influence the world. We will continue as long as we can resource our military."

"Thousands of our people are still dying for the war Your Excellency."

"The war is done Takeda. We have enough gold to control the world, enough of our people have died. We are talking to the Americans. You are to go to Taipei and meet with a Brigadier General called Bonner Fellers. He is the assistant of MacArthur. Prime Minister Suzuki has requested a meeting to discuss how we can bring an end to the war. They must allow us to retain the Philippines as part of any agreement. I would like it if we could keep Korea. Tell the American that Korea has been a Japanese protectorate since nineteen hundred and ten. The people consider themselves Japanese.

"The Americans are stupid, they think the war is about land and empire. Our spies have reported that the Americans have captured and tortured Major Khojima, General Yamashita's driver. I have instructed that Khojima should cooperate with the Americans and lead them to the twelve 'Golden Lily' sites that he knows. They will probably be able to penetrate six of the twelve sites, the other six will be too difficult, your engineers and experts have made the entrances invisible. They will access what to them is a vast amount of gold bullion, to us it is nothing. A small price to pay. You can use information as to how to access the gold in those sites as a carrot for the American donkey. For that information I require the absolute exoneration for all living members of the throne from any allegations or enquiries relating to war crimes. Freedom from any form or reparations from any country, company or person on the grounds that the war has bankrupted Japan and it has no reserves and the retaining of The Chrysanthemum Throne as a constitutional monarchy after the war has ended. "

"And what else am I asking for Your Excellency?"

"An end to the killing of our people. An end to this battle. It is a battle. For us the war will go on but in a different way. In a technological, economic way, we have enough wealth to lead the world. And remember Takeda, never use the word 'surrender'. I cannot, as the Emperor, contemplate surrender when I demand my people die rather than surrender. A negotiated end to the war is what we will agree to. If they object, remind them that every man in Japan is happy to die for the Emperor, our country, the Chrysanthemum Throne and if I decree it, every man that can lift a gun or a sword will die trying to kill an American. Remind them also that American Banks and Companies invested heavily in Japan before the war and that if they want to see any of their money back they need to think very carefully about who they imprison or execute."

Prince Takeda bowed. A soft gong sounded, a kneeling servant opened the door and the Emperor left the room. Prince Takeda left by the other door and walked the small distance to the small mansion set at the back of the palace estate. It was early summer and most of the cherry blossom had dropped from the trees. Only the last few petals remained, sweepers constantly scooping up dead flowers and leaves, almost as they dropped. One of the black double gates opened for him as he approached, he could see his young son and two younger daughters playing on the swings at the side of the house. A female servant stood close by hoping and praying that none of the children fell. He stood and watched them. It was as though they had a large basket full of laughter that got used up as you went through life. He couldn't remember the last time he had laughed. Thinking back may be it had been laughing at Benhameen waking up surrounded by gold coins, but that moment had passed quickly.

He walked over to them.

"Push me Daddy! Push me!" His son yelled.

"No push me daddy! Push me! Not him." His daughter shouted.

Daddy went behind them and pushed them both, their giggles and screams for more and higher took him away from it all.

Chapter. 13.

"Sit down Fellers, thanks for coming over so quickly. Sit down."

Brigadier General Bonner Fellers walked towards the massive wooden desk of General Douglas MacArthur and took one of the two seats. It was hot. Summer in the Philippines was always hot, large ceiling fans whirred the air around the spacious embassy office. The air smelt, not unpleasantly, of the Generals corn cob pipe.

"You're aware of the Jap operation called 'Golden Lily'?"

"Yes Sir, I am."

"Well, Lansdale and his OSS cronies have 'leant on' a Jap Major called Khojima, now, he was the driver for General Yamashita, who as you know has only just surrendered. Khojima has lead us to the twelve 'Golden Lily' sites that he knows of. We have accessed three of those sites and there's vast amounts of gold bullion bars stashed to the roof. More money than you or I can imagine. The President has directed that we keep stum about it as that amount of bullion would wreck the worlds markets and seriously devalue the dollar. Plus it will be very handy to have some collateral 'off the books' if you know what I mean."

MacArthur pushed out his feet, leant back in his chair and re-lit the pipe.

"I do Sir."

"This Major also let out that there are one hundred and seventy two sites in all, spread around the Philippines. Now, the Philippines are ours, never mind this independence talk, they can be as independent as they like but we have the money. We own the Philippines. The Commies won't get it and when we get Japan they won't get that either."

"Are the Japs suing for peace at the moment Sir?"

"They are Bonner, that's where you come in. You're going to Formosa, Taipei, there you'll hook up with a Japanese Royal Prince called Takeda.

"They're on their knees, the air and sea blockade has cut off their food and fuel, our firebombing campaign has destroyed over thirty cities. They are desperate for peace. The President wants access to all of those sites. He wants all the gold those Japs have systematically stolen from the nineteen thirties up to now. It's more gold than you can ever think of Bonner. We can't physically give it back to the countries it was taken from as it's all been resmelted, in Malaya, apparently, but that gold is ours."

"What if they won't play ball Sir?"

General Douglas MacArthur pushed back his chair.

"Then we'll use the A bomb. The Air force are desperate to try it for real."

Bonner Frank Fellers stood up, his Quaker parents had struggled with the decision to send him to West Point but figured that as an officer it was unlikely that he would have to personally fight or kill someone, they were comfortable with Bonner in an 'administrative role'.

"I've heard it's a terrible weapon Sir, a weapon that can kill years later with radiation sickness."

"If you don't want the job Bonner I'll send someone else but you're the Psy- Ops Jap expert."

"No. No. I'll do it Sir. When is it scheduled?"

"You'll fly out next Monday. Meet this Prince next Tuesday. The Embassy will arrange everything, you'll be ferried around by some of Chiang Kai Shek's people, he has a summer villa there."

"Sir?"

"Yes Bonner."

"Do the Japs know about the A bomb?"

"Don't know Bonner, but if they don't, you can tell em."

Brigadier Fellers was dismissed by the lighting of a pipe. He walked out of the light airy office, an armed guard on the door saluted. Bonner Fellers ignored him, in fact he didn't notice him. So deep in thought. This was Cairo all over again. He couldn't get over it. It was always there. He'd used a radio to transmit strategic information about the British plans in North Africa to Washington, they'd been intercepted and thousands had died at Tobruk and Gazala at the hands of Rommel's forces because of him. Every night it was there and now if he got it wrong again thousands more could die. Ambition came at a dreadful price for Bonner Frank Fellers.

The unmarked twin engined DC3 waited impatiently on the apron at Clark Airfield, its engines spluttering and coughing as they idled. The Jeep with just one passenger hurried towards the plane. It swung alongside the door and steps. A young woman in civilian clothes waited at the door. Bonner Fellers was dressed in a grey suit and a blue tie. Determined to put on a show he jumped from the jeep like the young man he wasn't then walked briskly over to the steps and up into the plane. The door immediately closed as the propellers bit into the hot noon time air. He had two hours to think about things again. He'd brought with him a leather briefcase, he didn't really know why, it just seemed as though a travelling Brigadier General should have one. In it was just a notebook, a couple of pencils and a fountain pen. This visit, this contact, didn't happen and wasn't recorded anywhere. If the plane crashed America would just lie.

The driveway after the black iron gates went on forever, a deep almost hidden valley that wound its way up and out. Two sentry posts either side of the gates were manned by Chinese soldiers. It was beautiful. A wide grass verge either side sprouted coconut palms every fifty metres. A verge of flowers separated the verge from the climbing jungled bank. Eventually the narrow road splayed out in front of a small deep amber coloured mansion where the grey Ford came to a halt.

Bonner Fellers was the first to arrive. He was greeted at the front by Soong Mei-Ling the elegant wife of Chiang Kai Shek and her two attendants, one of whom held a parasol to shield Mei-Ling from the late afternoon sun.

Bonner Fellers held out his hand. It was taken limply as though he was shaking the hand of an actress accustomed to adulation. Her smile was designed to flatter. He felt vulnerable. He was in a strange place with no support, no protection, no America.

The attraction was strong and immediate. Her eyes were like magnets, wherever he looked he was drawn irresistibly back to them, she was the same, whenever he glanced towards her she was looking at him. They had a whole relationship in a second.

"Good afternoon General, please come in and take a drink to refresh you. It's such an honour to have such a famous General in my simple house."

"Thank you Madame Chiang Kai Shek. It's an honour to be here and to meet you. I'm not actually a General, just a Brigadier General."

"You're too modest Mr. Fellers, a General is a General and that's it. Come, follow me into the reception lounge. My husband can't be here as he's busy on mainland China but he's asked me to convey his best wishes to you and that your meeting will be a successful one. A less effective Japan would be a huge relief to my husband if you know what I mean. He could concentrate then on saving China from the communists."

"We all share that wish and vision Madame Ch--------"

She stopped him in mid conversation.

"Please call me Mei-Ling General."

"Yes, Japan is a distraction my husband could do without." She smiled from a distance.

"If the Japanese Prince wishes it, do you want to dine with him?"

"Do you know if he is coming alone? Can he speak English OK or will he have interpreters with him?"

"I think like you General. He comes alone. We have only been asked to provide one bed for the night."

"If he wants to I would like that."

Madame Chiang Kai Shek gestured him to sit with her on the chaise lounge while they waited for a tray of fruit juices. She looked so serene, so controlled, so beautiful.

"How are things in the Philippines General. I hear that Japan is on it's knees because of your Navy and Air Force.?"

"It's difficult for me to answer your questions, if you understand me." Bonner Fellers took the opportunity to look directly into her eyes of the shrewd inquisitive captivating Mei-Ling.

"Of course! Of course. Please forgive me. I should not have asked you such a question. Do you have a wife and family General?"

General Fellers and Madame Chiang Kai Shek spoke about everything for at least thirty minutes. She was tactile, touching and stroking whenever their conversation allowed it. Never before had Bonner Fellers felt such immediacy. Madame Chiang was so intuitive around him that she knew what he was going to say after just a few words. He didn't want to stop. He wanted the words to draw them ever closer until it was impossible to separate them. To be as one with her.

"Now you must rest General, my maid will show you to your room."

"Thank you. Do you know what time The Prince is expected?"

"About six I think General. I will send someone up to your room when he arrives."

The room was sumptuous, the bed huge, the linen of the highest quality. The view from the heavily draped large window was just green with a hint of the sea far away. He was nervous as to the enormity of his mission. This was first contact between two countries at war. Everyone knew a process had to start but no one was to know how, where or when. He lay on the bed and sank deep into it. Soft down voluminous pillows yielded then gently supported his head. It was silent then sleep came.

Prince Tsuneyoshi Takeda arrived in a Rolls Royce, followed by a large Mercedes. Both were black. Prince Takeda had not wished it but the Emperor had ordered the two large cars shipped to Formosa along with the Prince and his support.. It had taken three days. Formosa had been colonised by Japan fifty years earlier but retained a degree of independence and although technically 'at war' with Chinese Nationalist led by the 'Generalissimo' there was an air of 'acceptable neutrality' when required. Sufficient to allow Chiang Kai Shek and his wife a discreet summer palace.

A servant from the following Mercedes rushed to open the door of the Rolls Royce, bowing as he did so. Prince Takeda was dressed in white military uniform complete with a red chrysanthemum. Madame Chiang waited at the front door dressed in a long pencil slim deep purple dress with a diamante lizard on the left collar. The broach was dazzling but she was more so. It was a beautiful evening.

Prince Takeda and Madame Chiang moved towards each other, both were smiling. She held out her hand expecting it to be kissed by the gracious Prince. He shook her hand.

"Good evening Madame Chiang. It is a pleasure to meet you. Thank you for allowing me to visit."

"Prince Takeda, it pleases me more than you can know to help in some small way to try and bring peace to our nations. I have seen too much of war and what it does to children and families. I do so hope your meeting with the American General will be productive. Please come in."

In the predominantly yellow reception lounge she gestured for him to sit down. He chose an elegant wingback armchair facing the large arched window. Servants and attendants were waved away. She sat on the chaise lounge and leant back against the arm her long legs pointing towards the Prince.

"Now, do tell me about the Emperor, how is he? He must be very worried. He's in a very difficult position a constitutional monarch, a sovereign and a direct descendant of a sun goddess. How does he cope with all that? Japan isn't very liked at the moment what with the Nanking thing and Pearl Harbour. He must struggle with it all."

"He is well Madame Chiang. He doesn't struggle, he has guidance from the ancient Buddhist monk Nichiren. He does get exasperated that the military and government sometimes do not see his vision but he is 'above the clouds'."

"Yesssss! precisely! I fully understand. There are always problems leading a nation or an army. There's always someone who thinks they know better but have no idea about breeding or lineage. Do take some refreshment Prince. There's fresh orange or pineapple juice. The water is mineral water from our own well here. It's very good for your health." Madame Chiang crossed her legs prominently displaying her right ankle and tiny foot.

"Dinner will be at seven o'clock Prince. The dining room is directly across the hall from this room. I would suggest you take a short rest. My staff will show you to your suite, it's on the first floor at the front."

Prince Takeda stood up as Madame Chiang left the room. She was so worldly, so sophisticated, so beautiful. The house was beautiful, the weather perfect, the furnishings, the best money could buy from all over the world. His thoughts raced back to that terrible celebration dinner in the tunnels. Pretending to laugh, to sing, to joke all the time knowing that he was about to end the life of thousands of humans, sons, fathers, uncles, lovers, grandfathers! God, the world had turned in disgust on Prince Asaka after the Nanking massacre, forcing the alcoholic Prince back to Tokyo. He had done the same only differently, he had killed thousands only quietly, yet here he was living at the highest level, about to have another dinner that could decide whether or not thousands lived or died. Surely there had to be a better way to world peace than war, conflict, theft, death and domination.

Chapter 14.

The blackness was so complete, so dense, that when a gun was fired the flash from the muzzle could be seen a long way away in other tunnels. Tunnels to the left and right. In the last few hours hours there had been an increase in the number of gunshots as the noise ricocheted to and passed his ears.

"I'm beginning to feel a bit drowsy and dizzy Fred. How about you?"

There was no reply. Charlie touched Fred's arm. "How about you?"

Fred's skin felt cold, even in the awful dark heat.

Chapter 15.

Bonner Fellers was first in the dining room. He'd showered, put on a clean shirt but wore the same tie. He wanted the first meeting with the Japanese Prince to be friendly, low key and informal so had decided not to wear a jacket. A waiter had offered him red or white wine as he sat on the high backed dining chair. He elected for water. It was not the time to dull or mellow one's senses.

The large cream and gold dining room door was opened by a Japanese uniformed soldier. Prince Takeda entered and the door closed.

Brigadier General Fellers immediately felt underdressed. Royal Prince Takeda was dressed immaculately in a full evening suit complete with a high collared bow tie. He stood up, offered a smile, his eyes and his hand. Prince Takeda stood behind a chair whilst his soldier pulled it out, dismissed the soldier and then took The General's hand, his eyes coming up to see the smile and friendly eyes.

"Good evening General Fellers. It is with hope that I meet you."

The handshake was firm and went on for several seconds.

"I have hope as well Prince Takeda. I really do. Please let us sit. The menu is splendid. I thank goodness for civilised people even when countries are less so."

Prince Takeda sat down and picked up the menu card, beside each card was a small hand bell to summon a waiter. A listening servant stood the other side of the closed doors.

"Do you drink wine Prince?"

"I do like a glass of red wine and of course Japanese Sake."

"We could share a bottle of red."

Prince Takeda looked up and into the eyes of Brigadier General Bonner Frank Fellers.

"Yes, let's do that General. Let's do that."

Takeda rang his bell. The wine was delivered on a silver tray in an exquisite cut glass decanter. Polish or Czech Fellers thought to himself.

"Now Prince Takeda what would you like to do? We can either 'cut to the chase' and discuss things whilst we eat or eat and then talk business later."

Prince Takeda took a sip of wine and wiped his lips with the napkin whilst he considered.

"I think we should eat and drink first General. I fear that if we 'cut to the chase' as you call it, first, the wine and food won't taste as good."

"A very good decision Prince. I concur. Now tell me, do you have family? Children, what's the house like where you live?" Both men sipped and smiled as they became accustomed to each other's presence in the lavish large dining room.

The food and its presentation was perfect. Prince Takeda suspected the ruthless touch of a woman had made it so. General Fellers had chosen beefsteak, Prince Takeda, sushi. When coffee came General Fellers chose the 'chaise longe' and Takeda the wingback chair.

"I have to say Prince that I find this war ghastly. America would rather conquer with commerce and money than bombs and guns."

The consumed wine had made both men more prone to speak truthfully.

"Yes I agree, my uncle, Prince Chichibu and I became very concerned a long time ago when the Emperor took up the teachings of Nichiren."

"Who on earth is 'Nichiren'?"

"A twelfth century Buddhist monk who held the belief that enlightenment could be achieved in this world and all that was required was for Japan to lead the way to it. He believes Nichiren speaks and acts through him."

"What does he want at the moment?"

"The Emperor wants nothing. He is a God, the sovereign of Japan, the constitutional head of the government and the military but he has no power."

"I and the leaders of America don't buy into that. We believe he is in fact the 'de facto' leader of Japan. An enviable position Prince, as a god, no one dare question him. If he expresses an opinion or wish it happens. If that action goes wrong he can just step back. Power without the responsibility or accountability. The only people who achieve that in the West are criminals and gangsters."

"Here, General we tend to work with our criminals and gangsters, they can have their uses."

"Cards on the table Prince. America requires full unconditional surrender of Japan issued by means of a verbal public transmission from the Emperor. He is the real leader of Japan and he must use those words 'unconditional surrender'. The restoration of all overseas possessions back to their indigenous peoples. Finally, access to all one hundred and seventy two 'Golden Lily' sites in the Philippines. We will let you keep the gold and treasure you have already stashed in Japan but my President wants that gold."

Prince Takeda's face had hardened, the family man had disappeared.

"I think you know General that all of those demands are totally unacceptable. Every man and boy soldier in Japan comes to the army more than willing to die for the Emperor. In fact they consider it a great honour for themselves and their family if they die in battle or die fighting. They die for the Emperor and Japan. They are not afraid of death. They are taught that they must never surrender, they must die. That is why you never take Japanese prisoners of war. The Emperor can never say the words you wish."

Prince Takeda reached over and emptied the wine glass.

"We must retain the Philippines. We have allowed you access to twelve of the sites through Major Khojima."

"What do you mean by that exactly? Major Khojima was tortured until he agreed to disclose the sites he had been to."

"Major Khojima is a Japanese Officer he would have died screaming. He would have not told you anything. Word was got to him from the Emperor to cooperate with you. The six sites you have managed to reverse engineer and access, give you, your President and General MacArthur untold unaccountable riches. You have the location of six other sites, all you have to do is work out how to find and extract the treasure. Tell your President not to be greedy, to be satisfied. There is enough bullion in those sites to totally devalue the dollar so be careful. We must keep the Philippines and Korea. Japan has controlled Korea since the eighteen hundreds. The people there consider themselves Japanese.

"We also require assurance that the immediate members of the Chrysanthemum Throne be exonerated from any war crimes enquiry or action or any form of reparation costs."

"As I said before Prince Takeda, power without responsibility, an enviable position."

"The Emperor is a God General. He is never wrong."

There was a silence.

"Takeda, your country is on its knees, there's an air blockade, a sea blockade, you have no fuel, food, medicines, supplies of any kind."

"Then behead us General but never think that we will die. The war is just a stone we step on in our path to world domination."

"Takeda, thousands of your innocent people are dying from our firebombing. It will go on. We have a special bomb, a terrible bomb, it can kill fifty to a hundred thousand people in one blast, can carry on killing through sickness months after it has exploded. Please! I am asking you to reconsider and report favourably to your 'God' as to what he must do. I'm sure we can deal with the war crimes issue, after all America invested heavily in Japan before the war and I'm sure our banks would be more than happy to see things return to normal. If it is as you say, just a step on Japan's journey then surely if there's a way to stop the killing of your people you must take it."

"I don't believe you have such a weapon General. No such weapon exists. It would take a mountain of explosives to kill so many people."

"I am not lying Takeda but it is up to you. I can only tell you what I know and do my best to stop this war. Goodnight Sir."

Brigadier General Bonner Fellers stood up and left the room.

Prince Takeda rang the bell then spoke. Within minutes the two black cars were waiting.

Bonner Fellers lay awake on the soft deep bed, his head spinning. Perhaps he shouldn't have left so abruptly, perhaps he should have tried longer, harder. All that had happened was he had laid down America's terms and the Prince had refused them. Hardly a successful outcome. Hardly a compromise. They must want peace otherwise tonight would not have happened. It made no sense to him. If they wanted peace, an end to the war, they surely must be ready to give something.

The wine had had no effect, the importance and tension of the dinner had somehow negated the usual effect of alcohol. Slowly he began to feel drowsy. Then came a gentle but powerful feminine knock at the door.

Madame Chiang joined Bonner Fellers at his breakfast table on the rear patio area of the house. He stood up as she approached. She wore gossamer thin lemon chiffon. Her hair was fashionably styled and perfectly coiffured, so much so that he wondered if she flew to Paris or New York to maintain it.

"Good morning General. I trust you slept well."

"Not too well Madame Chiang I had a few distractions." They looked into each other's eyes. It was an easy thing to do.

"Things didn't go too well last night. Suffice to say I fear a lot more people will die before the war is finished."

She looked at the General over her coffee cup, she ate nothing.

"The Japanese are very difficult General, very difficult! Let me get the maid to pack you some of these pastries for your journey back, apparently they're delicious."

"Tell me Madame Chiang, how did you manage to acquire and maintain such a magnificent house in a country you're supposed to be at war with?"

"Oh it's not really a war, just little local fights and land grabs. My sister is friendly with the wife of the Emperor's brother. All the Chinese who work here think we're Russian. Ironic really, seeing as my husband's real enemy is Mao and the communists."

"I wouldn't call 'Nanking' a little local fight."

Madame Chiang eased back in her chair.

"No you're right General. Nanking was terrible, both myself and my husband feel very bad about it but it was the correct strategic decision at the time. 'Run away to fight another day' would be the best description. Abandoning seven thousand of our troops to almost certain death would be the worst."

"They say that over one hundred thousand innocent civilians were raped and killed at the hands of an out of control Japanese army. I fear the Japanese have no regard for the lives of ordinary people."

"That is the way of all the world General. If you are rich mainly you will be OK. If you have nothing and are in the wrong place at the wrong time it is highly likely that you will die and no one will really care."

"Does the Emperor care?"

"From what I've heard he doesn't know about Nanking. All he knows is that Prince Asaka has been recalled back to Tokyo for 'health' reasons. I suspect the Generals and senior officers who were below him at Nanking will be tried for war crimes and will almost certainly be executed. That is what I have heard."

"What are we going to do about last night Mei-Ling?"

"General, sometimes we are simply animals driven by nature we have to obey, we have no choice nature is so strong but circumstances steer us. Yesterday they steered us together for a moment, today they will steer us apart forever. It is the way of our world General. The way things are."

Tears moistened her eyes. General Fellers stood up to take out a handkerchief from his jacket pocket, wiped her eyes then placed it into her hand before leaving.

Chapter 16.

"Damn it Fellers. Couldn't you have brought me something positive from this meeting. Something I could use. Something I could at least talk to the President about."

General MacArthur sat down at his desk with his hat on. Taking it off was an inconsequential second to lighting his pipe.

"Sir we're not dealing with human minds as we perceive them. They're different, they consider dying an honour. They will literally fight to the last man, woman and child."

"So what are your thoughts Fellers?"

"We need to get to the Emperor. From what I gather the Japanese government and military are very selective about what he gets to know. He is probably the only person who could end the war. The government are struggling to control the military, parts of which are out of control and acting independently."

"And 'unconditional surrender'?"

"There's a problem with that as every Jap soldier believes surrender is dishonourable, not only to himself but to his family so he either dies fighting or commits suicide. The idea of the Emperor surrendering is just incomprehensible. They also want all of the Royal Family, The Chrysanthemum Throne, to be protected from any allegations of war crimes on the grounds that they had no real power or influence on Japan's actions."

"What about the Golden Lily gold? Will he play ball on that?"

"No Sir. Prince Takeda told me that Khojima was permitted to disclose those twelve sites by the Emperor who considered it a sacrificial act to keep us busy. He says that there is enough bullion in those sites to destabilise the dollar and that we could become very rich men."

General MacArthur rocked back in his chair put his feet up on the desk and thought deeply as he re-lit his pipe. He bellowed at the door.

"Sergeant! Coffee!"

"What about the 'A' bomb? Presumably you warned him about that? They're set to drop it in three days time unless I come up with something positive and at the moment Fellers I've got nothing."

"He didn't believe we had such a weapon, or so he said."

"And what about you Fellers? Did you believe him or not?"

"I believed him Sir. I can't understand why we're using such a terrible thing when they're obviously beaten or they wouldn't be talking to us. It's just a matter of how we can manage the end so as the Emperor and Japan don't lose face."

"I don't give a damn about the Emperor or Japan. I suspect it's payback time for Pearl Harbour, it's certainly payback time for me and Bataan, I really didn't appreciate being kicked out of the Philippines, plus the boffins want to try it out." The General finally took off his hat as the coffee came on a tray.

"Look Fellers. You're the Jap Psy-ops expert, where are they exactly?"

"I think they're on their knees because of our blockades but neither the government nor the army can call a halt, only the Emperor can do that and I'm not sure how well informed he is."

"That's a difficult one Fellers. If the Emperor is the only guy with the power to stop the war it could be said that he was the only guy with the power to start it, or at least stop it from starting, so there could be problems when it comes to responsibility for war crimes and from what I gather there are plenty of them."

"Abolish the throne Sir, except for the Emperor and his wife. That way we're seen to be taking action but leaving 'their God' in place. We don't have to fight the Japanese nation forever."

"I'll think about that when the time comes. What was the place like in Formosa?"

"A very discreet beautiful mansion Sir. Just perfect."

"And the host?"

"Like the mansion Sir." General MacArthur's eyes smiled as he looked over the desk.

"What about Prince Takeda, did you like him?"

"I did Sir, a very intelligent well informed man."

"Mmmm! Shame about the 'Golden Lily' sites, if they'd handed those over I think the President would have gone for a conventional end."

"So it's the money or their lives is it Sir?"

"'Fraid so Fellers! 'Fraid so! OK, got to get this report off to the President, I'll see you at the planning meeting this afternoon."

Brigadier Bonner Fellers left the room heading towards his staff car.

Chapter 17

Takeda lay on the hard teak bed thinking. Wind was billowing the curtains from the partially opened door that lead out to the flowers, plants and seats of the paved place where he ate breakfast. Beside him was his wife. Still sleeping. There was no dividing pillow between them.

A quiet gloved knock came at the other door, normally Mitsuko would respond but she was asleep. He arose went over and opened the door, a servant stood with head bowed offering a silver tray with a telegram on it addressed to Royal Prince Takeda. The imperial Palace Tokyo.

Prince Takeda took the telegram, dismissed the servant and went back into the bedroom.

"Prince Takeda, we can save thousands of lives if you can persuade the Emperor to hand over the 'Golden Lily' maps. Please consider. - Bonner Fellers."

He re read the telegram, save thousands of lives from what? The firebombing had already taken tens if not hundreds of thousands of lives, so what did this mean? What was the point? He knew the house servant would be waiting outside the closed door so he shouted "No reply".

It was eleven am. Prince Takeda waited in the Breakfast Room of the Palace. The atmosphere in the palace was tense. The military, especially the young officers had got wind that the Emperor was taking steps to end the war and didn't like it. The carpet firebombing of Japanese towns and cities by the Americans had caused catastrophic loss of life as fires ripped through the flimsy wood and paper neighbourhoods. Food, fuel and medicines were running out. The Emperor was considering surrendering. The army wanted to carry on fighting. To win or to die fighting but not to surrender. It was rumoured he was afraid to leave the palace for fear of assassination. He was worried the Army would invade the palace. Inside the palace it was still quiet and calm as the soft gong preceded the opening of the doors. Prince Takeda bowed towards the Emperor.

"What news Takeda?" The Emperor was dressed in a western style suit, gleaming black leather shoes and a grey silk tie. His moustache and thick gold rimmed glasses just made him look like the serious deeply burdened man he was.

"It is not good Your Excellency."

"Come Takeda, let's sit down at the table." The Emperor clapped his hands and two servants immediately ran in to pull out the chairs.

"Now, what did the American General say?"

"He said." There was a pause. "They had a new special bomb that could kill tens of thousands of people in one blast and that they were preparing to use it soon unless you comply with their terms. In particular the 'Golden Lily' sites"

"And do you believe that Takeda?"

"I told the American General that I didn't believe him but deep down I did. He had an honest round kind face and truthful eyes."

"I cannot disclose those sites Takeda, you know that. They are the future for all our descendants. It is the means we will need to rebuild our country into a new and dynamic nation. I cannot do that."

"They want you to broadcast to the nation a speech that includes the words 'unconditional surrender'. They want us to relinquish possession of all our overseas possessions including the Philippines, Manchuria and Korea."

"As you say Takeda, not good news."

"I fear it is a dreadful trap your Excellency. The military want to carry on fighting. Only you can instruct Japan to stop fighting, stop the war. If you do that the Americans will say that only you had the power to start the war or rather the power to stop it starting. They will come after you, come after us, the members of the Chrysanthemum Throne."

There was a commotion. Prince Takeda and the Emperor turned to look at the far door. There were raised voices and movement of the large heavy doors as though someone was trying to come in and someone was trying to stop them.

The Emperor was visibly alarmed. Was it the military storming the palace? Was he about to be assassinated?

Prime Minister Suzuki burst into the room. He was an elderly man. The exertions had left him breathless. Still wearing shoes he came over to the Emperor and bowed.

"Please excuse my behaviour and unannounced arrival your Excellency but I have grave news you must be aware of."

The Emperor was not amused. He had never before experienced an unsolicited approach. Admiral Suzuki had not been his preferred choice for Prime Minister but other more favoured officers had declined fearing assassination should they be in office at the time of surrender. Kantaro Suzuki had a kindly face and a fair attitude. He had opposed the war with America from it's onset.

The Emperor glanced over at Takeda for support.

"Go ahead with your report Prime Minister." The Emperor was curt and formal.

For all his years Suzuki's delivery was breathless like a nervous child.

"Your Excellency, I have to report there has been a huge catastrophic explosion above Hiroshima this morning. Reports say that the whole city centre has disappeared and everything else for miles has been flattened and burnt. Early estimates are that there are more than fifty thousand people dead and thousands more seriously injured. The military close to Hiroshima say they have never seen or experienced anything like it before. It is beyond belief." His breathing was still short and rapid.

There was silence.

"You were right Takeda, your General was not lying." The Emperor turned towards Suzuki.

"Prime Minister, thank you for your correct assessment of the urgency and your determination to deliver this information to me. Please ensure that as much assistance as humanly possible is directed towards assisting the surviving people of Hiroshima." There was a silence. " Goodbye."

Prime Minister Kantaro Suzuki bowed and moved towards the door he had struggled through five minutes before.

When he had gone the Emperor turned to Prince Takeda.

"Do you think that is it Prince Takeda? Do you think they had only one of these 'special' bombs or do you think they have more? If they have more will they use them to wipe out our country Takeda, - our home?"

"I cannot answer your questions your Excellency, I don't know the answers. I think if we give them the maps to the 'Golden Lily' sites they would not destroy us."

"I can never do that Takeda. They are our future. The whole reason our nation has suffered and died over the last twenty years. I will die before I do that."

Takeda thought before speaking.

"Perhaps you should consider the tens of thousands of your subjects who may die if you don't."

It was a bad day for Emperor Hirohito. First there had been the unannounced, unscheduled intrusion by the Prime Minister and now his words were being challenged by a trusted Prince of the Chrysanthemum Throne.

A soft gong sounded as the Emperor turned towards his door.

Chapter 18.

Admiral Kodama was a gangster. Before the war he had controlled rackets in Shanghai that were anything but peaceful. Drugs, prostitution, blackmail, kidnap, extortion. His hand was in and on everything. Above all Kodama was an ultra nationalist, his support and donations to the Chrysanthemum Throne guaranteed him favour with the Emperor. The Emperor guaranteed him high military rank. He controlled the Navy as well as the underworld. He controlled them both very well.

"Kodama, I need to get to the Philippines as quickly as possible and as discreetly as possible. Can you do that?" Prince Takeda spoke quietly into the phone in his house.

"The Philippines are occupied by the Americans Prince Takeda. Are you running away? Leaving Japan? Deserting the Emperor?"

"No, I'm trying to save Japan. I will need you to get me back - safely I hope. "

"I am happy to hear that Kimsu." Hearing the word 'Kimsu' took him immediately back to the hot quiet nights listening to Ben breathing next to him. Knowing that when he awoke he could look at the beautiful innocent young boy who did everything for him with a smile.

"I have a captured American Motor Torpedo boat, it is very fast, it was damaged but we've repaired it. It's still in American colours."

"Will it make it there and back at high speed on the fuel?"

"We'd have to carry some extra drums but it would be OK."

"How long will it take at top speed?"

"About three days."

"I'd need to land close to Aparri in the north and I'd need transport, a car or Jeep."

"Do not worry Kimsu. We have many friends in the Philippines, many people do not like the Americans. What time do you wish to leave?"

"How soon can the boat be ready?"

"Three to four hours."

"Say six o'clock this evening then."

"It will be ready Sir."

The telegram read. - "I am coming to give you the maps - ETA Three days, please wait. - Tsuneyoshi Takeda - Royal Prince - Chrysanthemum Throne."

"What do think Fellers? Are they bluffing? Playing for time?"

General Douglas MacArthur tapped out his pipe on the inside of the yellow metal waste paper bin and picked up his coffee cup.

"I don't think so Sir, surely it's worth waiting three days, they're going to surrender soon, they have to, so it's just those maps that we need."

The General rocked back in his chair.

"OK Fellers, we'll give it three days, just hope you're right, from what the photo intelligence guys say there's nothing left of Hiroshima, must have been one hell of a bang. The photos are coming over this afternoon, come by and look. Got to brief the President about a second drop so I'll mention our arrangement. Not sure about Truman, not a patch on Roosevelt. That's private mind, just between you and me."

Prince Takeda kissed his wife and children goodbye as though leaving for the office. He was dressed very casually, long light brown slacks, sandals and an open necked short sleeved cream shirt. He carried no money and nothing that would identify him. A Navy Jeep was waiting outside the gates. The driver stood to attention and saluted as Takeda got in. It took fifteen silent minutes to reach the dockside.

It bobbed up and down restlessly as the warm chaotic breezes played with the waves. The fenders squeaked and groaned. The craft was light grey and dark red at the water lIne. A painted timber and fabric shutter covered the hole where the front gun had been. Fresh paint on the starboard side hull marked the wounds of bullets that had ripped into her. Four Japanese sailors leaning on the gangplank rails sprang to attention as the lights of the jeep slowed towards them. Takeda saluted walked aboard and headed towards the small bridge. A young officer greeted him with a bow as the gangplank was shipped and the deep throb of the engines intruded on the quiet air.

It was dark as they moved swiftly out of the harbour, once out, the engines were let loose to lift the bow out of the now black sea and push it towards the Philippines. Takeda was nervous, almost scared, going into a hostile country controlled by the enemy. An enemy more than prepared to slaughter thousands of his countrymen for gold. His thoughts led to his instructions from the Emperor and his own actions. There was no difference. All for gold. It would be good to see Ben, if only for a few moments.

It was not like the 'Huzi Maru': this vessel banged and crashed through the solid sea, bucking and jumping like a young horse. It was uncomfortable, Takeda and the crew had to hang on to something.

"Sir, if you will accompany me I will guide you to your cabin. I am sorry it is not very large or comfortable." The young captain focused his gaze towards the collar of Takeda's shirt.

Holding on to rails and doors Takeda followed the Captain off the bridge and down below to a welcome bunk. The whole ship smelt of diesel oil with the occasional smell of cooking.

The American diesel engines roared all night and all day. Both the Captain and Takeda were worried about being challenged by the US. Navy or spotted by the Airforce, but their speed took them safely past ships, quickly leaving maritime traffic on a distant horizon.

Takeda had plenty of time to dwell on what he was doing. Was it treason.? Was he a traitor to the Emperor or a saviour to Japan? By handing over the maps would he condemn Japan to a century of servitude, a poor smashed country without the means to rebuild itself? No! There was enough bullion and treasure hidden away in Japan, in the vaults under the palace, in the caves in the mountains to rebuild the country. This was saving thousands of lives. Did the Emperor really want to use the wealth for the country? Or was it simply to ensure the continuing wealth and dominance of the Chrysanthemum Throne? Who could say? Only time could answer that question. Was he really doing this for Japan? For the people? Or for himself? To once more be close to Ben, the boy who lit up every corner of his being. Who had made his life fun.

His Dahoum. Dahoum had died before Takeda's boyhood hero T. E. Lawrence could get back to him. Was Ben dead? Had he been killed for gold? Joined the countless thousands who had died for gold? The powerful boat smashed into another big wave that shuddered the craft. It was like skipping over rocks.

It was just dark at the end of the second day when the engines slowed and the boat became gentle. Takeda left the small cabin and headed for the bridge. Somehow he could smell the Philippines, it was a soft, round smell, different to Japan.

"Why have we slowed Captain?"

The captain stood at rigid attention.

"Sir, we are approaching Aparri. We have made excellent time due to favourable currents and winds. My instructions are to land you by dinghy at a small inlet some five kilometers away on the western side of the town and then wait for your return. Should you not return the same night I am to select an uninhabited island, conceal my ship if possible, then return the next night. I have been ordered to do that for three days and nights, then return to Tokyo with or without you."

"Thank you Captain, that is a sensible plan. Now what about transport once I land?"

"Sir. Admiral Kodama has arranged that." Takeda wondered how on earth Kodama had managed to do that.

It was a calm warm black night, the rubber dinghy just caressed the side of the fast grey boat as they bumped together. Two sailors held two ropes as Takeda climbed down the rope net. The rower in the dinghy hesitated. Normally he would assist a passenger, hold his hand or arm as he got in but this was a royal prince, a relative of a living god. No he couldn't touch him. The beach was only one hundred meters away, it took a few minutes for the skilful rower to reach it. Takeda was able to jump out without getting his feet wet. There, behind the trees was a flash of light and a low whistle. Takeda made his way towards it.

The car was a large black Studebaker. Takeda could tell the driver and his assistant were Japanese, their faces were harder, flatter and whiter than Philippino's. Their hair seemed thicker and more languid with a wave in it. No they were definitely Japanese. Takeda directed them towards the village where Ben's father lived. Would he be there? Had he married? Was he still alive? Ben was on his mind now, more than the maps. It shouldn't have been like that, but it was.

It took nearly two hours travelling slowly along the dark country roads. Since the Americans had reoccupied and the Japanese war was nearly over, security was slack. They saw only one American patrol en route and that paid scant attention as they passed. The Studebaker was an American car.

Then they were there.

The tin and wooden hut was just as it had been, the dark night hiding it's poverty. Inside a light glimmered.

Royal Prince Takeda walked towards the leaning corrugated tin panel that served as a door at night and gently tapped on it. The panel was moved aside by Ben's father. He looked quite sinister with his eye patch and the moving light of the gently hissing paraffin lamp. A dirt floor, a cheap wooden chest of drawers that acted as a family shrine, three repaired wooden chairs and a plastic table. He could see Ben asleep in a hammock. Brown, lithe, thin, supple, his hair trailing down the side of his face and neck, his skin still shone with happiness and willingness to oblige. It was like an aura. Ben's father didn't know what to say and gestured for him to come in. He was used to seeing this man in a magnificent white military uniform surrounded by generals. Now, here he was, in drab ordinary clothes, just a black car waiting behind him.

Kimsu spoke softly.

"Ben, Benhameen wake up!" He shook the sides of the hammock but it just made it swing a little.

Ben's father spoke in Tagalog to wake his son.

Prince Takeda could see absolute shock spread over Ben's face as he emerged from sleep. He sprang from the hammock.

"Kimsu! Kimsu! Is it you or am I dreaming?" He looked over to his father and then back.

"It is me Benhameen, you are not dreaming. I am so glad to see you safe and well."

Ben dropped to his knees before his prince and looked up directly into his eyes.

"Why are you here Kimsu? Are the Japanese coming back?"

"No Ben the Japanese are never coming back." Prince Takeda paused. "Not with an army anyway, maybe as friends sometime in the future. I am here for the maps, I want you to dig them up for me. I will hold a light."

Ben's face immediately drained of blood, his jaw dropped and within seconds his kneeling body was shaking uncontrollably.

Prince Takeda put his arms around the now sobbing boy. Between the sobs and tears he spoke.

"I cannot do it Kimsu. I cannot do what you ask. I so want to do it, I want to do everything for you for the rest of my life but I cannot do what you ask."

Ben's cheeks, chin and the earth floor immediately below his bowed convulsing head were wet and stained.

Takeda was calm and gentle, stroking his head. Two large moths fought over the hissing lamp.

"Tell me Benhameen. Tell me why you can't get me the maps."

Ben's sobbing slowly stopped as he made an effort to speak.

"Prince Takeda, Kimsu. I did as you said. I put the satchel in a suitcase and buried it very deep, as deep as I could but two months ago there was a typhoon and I didn't know! I didn't know but the floods were very high and came way past the Banyan tree. The water lifted the suitcase up to just below the ground. Then the pigs ate everything Kimsu. The suitcase was made of cardboard Kimsu, I didn't know. They ate the suitcase and your satchel and the maps. All I found was the metal buckles. I keep them in my box. I didn't expect to see you for thirty years and may be, if I was lucky I would die before then. I have failed you Kimsu! I have failed you. If you want to kill me, shoot me, chop off my head, torture me, then take me KImsu. I deserve it."

"Stand up Benhameen, Stand up."

Prince Takeda clasped the sobbing shaking boy's head to his shoulder and stroked his hair.

"Benhameen you have helped me more than you will ever know, helped me to cope with doing a foul despicable thing. Killing thousands of people for a dull heavy metal. In your eyes I saw all the happiness in all the stars. In your smile I saw all the love that should have been, that I took away. Without you to love I would have failed to do what the Emperor had bid me and would have died. You have saved my life Benhameen. Now sleep, when you wake, it will be just as a dream. I was never here."

Now there was only one large moth fluttering and crashing into the hot light. The other was dead on the floor.

Prince Takeda kissed Benhameen's head then turned and left.

"Where to Excellency?"

"Back to the boat."

The journey back was fast but not as urgent and hard as the race to the Philippines. The young Captain concentrated on avoiding everything. The sailors emptied five forty five gallon drums of fuel into the tanks as the willing diesels throbbed. Prince Takeda stayed in the small cabin, not really caring if he made it back safely or died. He ate what was served to him but couldn't remember what it was. Nine months before he had struggled to relegate Ben to the unreachable past and now he had to do it again.

Chapter 19

"Anything Fellers?"

"Nothing Sir. Nothing."

"Bit of a disappointment to you Fellers I'd say."

For a five star General Douglas MacArthur was quite sensitive to those immediately around him. His battered and stained field cap had been thrown onto the desk in his urgency to light his pipe. He was still wearing his sunglasses.

" Yes Sir, I thought when that telegram came we were making progress. That there was movement and we wouldn't have to use it anymore. Yes Sir. I am very disappointed."

"Sit down Bonner, don't beat yourself up about it, every soldier that ever was has recriminations about something."

"Sergeant two coffees and get me a link with the White House if you can."

"Takeda. Where on earth have you been? No one's seen you for six days. There's been another one. Have you heard?" Prince Chichibu was just leaving Mitsuko at the gates of Takeda's small mansion.

"I had to go away for a while. Where?"

"Nagasaki. They're saying that at least eighty thousand people are dead. Can you imagine that, eighty thousand people gone in an instant. It's a horrendous horrible nightmare."

"I know nightmares very well Chichibu."

Prince Chichibu gave his nephew a strange look.

"Come, we need to go and see the Emperor right now. This needs to be stopped. We have to surrender or they'll be nothing left of our country or it's people."

"Give me a little time to wash and put on my uniform. I cannot see the emperor like this.

Princes Takeda and Chichibu sat together in the back of the black Rolls Royce as it glided the short distance to the Imperial Palace.

"Do you think he knows?"

"I don't know. I heard about two o'clock from Tojo, he's still close to the military and gets all the important information. Where've you been anyway? It was a Navy jeep that brought you home so I assume somewhere on a boat."

"I went to see the family of Navy Captain Honda, I'm having trouble getting over blowing the entrance on the last site. Thousands of people were in there Chichibu, as you well know. Captain Honda was a good friend. I feel terrible about it." It was a partial truth used as a lie.

"It's not you Takeda, you had no choice. The Emperor wanted it."

"That doesn't help at night time, knowing that my night will finish but their's won't."

The Emperor knelt facing the predominantly golden shrine to Nichiren chanting the mantra *'Nam Myoho Renge Kyo'*. Princes Takeda and Chichibu entered the room from the rear and stood silently waiting until he had finished.

Emperor Hirohito sensed their presence, rose and turned towards them. Bowing, the Princes moved towards him across the ancient wooden floor.

"There has been another disaster your Excellency. Eighty thousand feared dead in Nagasaki."

The Emperor held up his hand.

"I know, I am aware. This slaughter must stop. The young Army Officers are threatening to storm the palace, to kill me, to assassinate me. They fear I will surrender and they are right. I cannot allow our nation, our people, to be destroyed. Only I have the power to stop it but I fear they will stop me if I leave the palace to make an announcement to the nation. Everything has changed now. The Americans have the power to totally remove our lineage, our history, our people. I have to do this but I don't know how."

"Your Excellency. Prince Chichibu and I have discussed this and it would be possible for you to make a phonograph record and for that record to be smuggled out of the palace and played to the nation."

There was a long silence.

"What would I say?"

"We would write your speech Excellency. It will not include the words 'unconditional surrender'; It will not say anything about the 'Golden Lily' deposits."

There was another silence.

"The 'Golden Lily' maps Takeda, are they safe?"

It was the question Takeda was dreading. He bowed his head.

"The maps are lost your Excellency. They are lost to everyone and us. A natural disaster took them away from us."

The silence was eternal.

"Good, that is good Takeda. Now the world has changed that is good."

"Do it. Arrange it quickly Prince Takeda. We cannot suffer another explosion."

That afternoon a phonograph recording was made by the Emperor in the great library of the palace. The record was smuggled out in a laundry basket.

The voice of the Emperor of Japan, the living god, was heard by his people for the first time over the radio on the fourteenth of August nineteen forty five. He spoke in formal court Japanese. Not many ordinary Japanese could understand it.

TO OUR GOOD AND LOYAL SUBJECTS:

After pondering deeply the general trends of the world and the actual conditions obtaining in our empire today, we have decided to effect a settlement of the present situation by resorting to an extraordinary measure.

We have ordered our government to communicate to the governments of the United States, Great Britain, China and the Soviet Union that our empire accepts the provisions of their joint declaration.

To strive for the common prosperity and happiness of all nations as well as the security and well-being of our subjects is the solemn obligation which has been handed down by our imperial ancestors and which lies close to our heart.

Indeed, we declared war on America and Britain out of our sincere desire to ensure Japan's self-preservation and the stabilization of East Asia, it being far from our thought either to infringe upon the sovereignty of other nations or to embark upon territorial aggrandizement.

But now the war has lasted for nearly four years. Despite the best that has been done by everyone – the gallant fighting of the military and naval forces, the diligence and assiduity of our servants of the state, and the devoted service of our one hundred million people – the war situation has developed not necessarily to Japan's advantage, while the general trends of the world have all turned against her interest.

Moreover, the enemy has begun to employ a new and most cruel bomb, the power of which to do damage is, indeed, incalculable, taking the toll of many innocent lives. Should we continue to fight, not only would it result in an ultimate collapse and obliteration of the Japanese nation, but also it would lead to the total extinction of human civilization

Such being the case, how are we to save the millions of our subjects, or to atone ourselves before the hallowed spirits of our imperial ancestors? This is the reason why we have ordered the acceptance of the provisions of the joint declaration of the powers.

We cannot but express the deepest sense of regret to our allied nations of East Asia, who have consistently cooperated with the Empire towards the emancipation of East Asia.

The thought of those officers and men as well as others who have fallen in the fields of battle, those who died at their posts of duty, or those who met with untimely death and all their bereaved families, pains our heart night and day.

The welfare of the wounded and the war-sufferers, and of those who have lost their homes and livelihood, are the objects of our profound solicitude.

The hardships and sufferings to which our nation is to be subjected hereafter will be certainly great. We are keenly aware of the inmost feelings of all of you, our subjects. However, it is according to the dictates of time and fate that We have resolved to pave the way for a grand peace for all the generations to come by enduring the unendurable and suffering what is insufferable.

Having been able to safeguard and maintain the Kokutai.*, We are always with you, our good and loyal subjects, relying upon your sincerity and integrity.*

Beware most strictly of any outbursts of emotion which may engender needless complications, or any fraternal contention and strife which may create confusion, lead you astray and cause you to lose the confidence of the world.

Let the entire nation continue as one family from generation to generation, ever firm in its faith in the imperishability of its sacred land, and mindful of its heavy burden of responsibility, and of the long road before it.

Unite your total strength, to be devoted to construction for the future. Cultivate the ways of rectitude, foster nobility of spirit, and work with resolution – so that you may enhance the innate glory of the imperial state and keep pace with the progress of the world.

Tokyo, August 14, 1945

Chapter 20.

Princess Nagako addressed her husband as he was being dressed by his courtiers. There were three of them. None of them had ever looked into the eyes of the Emperor. His dressing room was as large as his bedroom and had interconnecting doors with Princess Nagako's chambers. Like most of the rooms in the palace it was furnished with elegant French furniture.

"Why are you travelling to meet this American General. The Emperor never visits a mortal person. They are granted a meeting here in the palace."

"Because my dear wife I do not wish this unsophisticated American to see our home, besides which, he would not be alone, there would be aides who would try to look everywhere. No It is better this way."

The Emperor sat on a large upright chair whilst the courtier put on his shoes. They were gleaming black leather. As he stood up he waived the courtiers away.

"The American does not understand. The war has served its purpose. The Chrysanthemum Throne has the means now to grow Japan according to the teachings of Nichiren, like children who have to be taught how to behave we will dominate the world with our social order, our intelligence, our history, but not our guns."

Princess Nagako smiled at her stiff, serious husband.

"Please be careful, they may arrest you for the war. I may never see you again." She stroked the arm of his morning suit. A Courtier entered with a black top hat and bowed as he handed it to Emperor Hirohito.

"I am ready." The courtier glanced over to the door and a soft gong sounded as the oak double doors silently opened. A team of courtiers silently fussed around moving on silent cloth feet the only sound being resonance of the Emperor's hard leather heels on the polished wooden floor.

The large black Rolls Royce was sandwiched between two black Mercedes saloons that already contained his aides and guards.

The smiles, handshakes, photographs, bows and pleasantries over, General Douglas MacArthur and Emperor Hirohito sat in the large day room of the Chancery building, between them sat Katsuzo the imperial translator.

There could be no greater contrast. Hirohito stiff and formal in his grey and black morning suit. MacArthur relaxed and casual with an open shirt and no tie. MacArthur blunt, direct, forceful but respectful. Hirohito in a different place, protected by formality.

The two men remained standing as people left the room, eventually it was just the three of them. The interpreter blended in with the room, almost inconspicuous, the correct distance and position from his Emperor.

"My countrymen and the British want you and your male family members prosecuted for war crimes."

"And what do you want General?"

"What my President doesn't want is communism."

"Then you have a problem General. Russia is already communist and China is sliding towards it."

"We aim to stop it by supporting democratic governments in countries like Japan and the Philippines."

Emperor Hirohito stood stiff and still in the spacious day room of MacArthur's billet. It was eleven in the morning, His black motorcade waited outside the Embassy building.

"I want the gold Emperor. My President wants access to all the 'Golden Lily' sites in the Philippines."

"The maps are lost General. Lost to you and lost to me. Even if you had them it would take you a hundred years to open them up."

"And how do I know you're not lying? If you can't give me the gold, why should I protect you and your family from war crimes allegations and investigations? You've just stopped this war, so people will think you could have stopped it before it started. They will think you are the power of Japan." MacArthur looked directly into the face and eyes of Emperor Hirohito. "Do you mind if I smoke?"

"General, before the war America invested heavily in Japan. Your banks have a lot of debt resting here. If you want to recover any of it, it will be in your interest not to pursue too vigorously your investigations. Also you and your President have not revealed to the world your colossal bullion recoveries made by Santy Romano, Edward Lansdale and yourself. I and the rest of the world have not heard anything about the twelve sites I gave you through Major Khojima. Disclosure of that information would perhaps make people think that something dishonest, perhaps criminal, was going on."

"Look Emperor, I have no desire to go after you or your immediate family but myself, America and its allies must be seen to do something. Now, one of my aides, an expert in Japanese psychology has suggested that we formally and legally disband the Chrysanthemum Throne with the exception of yourself, your wife and immediate heirs. That way your country will retain their loyalty to you but the world will see that we have acted."

The Emperor of Japan uncomfortably lowered himself into one of the chairs putting both hands on the curved wooden arms.

"You can have Generals Adachi and Yamashita and ex prime minister Tojo. They will take full responsibility for the war and its military failures. They have indicated to the Imperial Palace that they would prefer to die rather than dishonour the throne or live in shame. I will agree to your suggestion to the dissolution of the Chrysanthemum Throne. Who suggested that General?"

"One of my staffers, Brigadier General Bonner Fellers. Why?"

"Only a man with vision and faith would suggest such a thing. It is, for you, the best possible outcome. Destroy the throne and you would condemn America to an eternity of insurgency. Now I have a suggestion for you, not as a General, not as an American, but as a man and a father. First let me assure you of the total loyalty of my interpreter."

Douglas MacArthur moved his hat along the desk and sat on the corner.

"As you are aware General, we managed to ship large quantities of bullion to Japan before your military blockaded Japan. The British and Dutch had moved their gold bullion reserves to Singapore and Jakarta thinking it would be safe should the war in Europe go badly. We were able to access that gold, some of which has been moved to Switzerland. I would like to suggest that you and I create an account in Switzerland into which I will deposit a considerable amount of gold bullion, only you and I and our direct descendant heirs will be signatories. The deposit will remain mine but the interest, which will be more than enough to maintain any future family you may have, will keep them in luxury for the foreseeable future. For centuries General."

General Douglas MacArthur glanced over at the interpreter.

Emperor Hirohito noticed his disquiet.

"Silence is guaranteed General."

"You are trying to bribe me Emperor. Trying to buy your way out of being indicted for war crimes."

"No General. I am offering you the chance of peace in Japan, a chance for your businesses and commerce to recover its losses and a chance for you to ensure the happiness of your family for a very long time. Be sure that your country will discard you as soon as you change from being an asset to a liability. The only allegiance you really have is to your son, your grandchildren and their continued success and happiness."

"I'll need time to think about that."

"There is no time General. When I walk out of your door the opportunity is lost. For me it is a guarantee that you will honour your words, that you will work to re-establishing the ruling families of Japan. For you it is the only useful thing you will take away from Japan."

"What do you intend to call this fund Emperor?"

"When I am dead I will be called the 'Showa' Emperor. We will call it the 'Showa Fund.'"

Emperor Hirohito and General MacArthur shook hands. The interpreter turned away.

Emperor Hirohito left the room. The double doors opened for him. A servant handed him his top hat.

Chapter 21

Prince Yaswhiko Asaka the Emperor's brother sat on his own the other side of the room sitting quietly on the thin legged chair. There were seven people in the ornate room. The three other brothers, Mikasa and Takamatsu and Chichibu and three male cousins, Takeda, Tarama, Otowa.

It was the same. The same time of year, the same room, the same chilled weather as thirteen years ago. They waited for the Emperor. Before he had been ebullient, confident, brusque. Now things were different, the hummed conversation sensed it.

The gong sounded, a kneeled servant swung open the doors. An older Emperor entered. Like before there was no introduction, no filial friendship.

"The war is done. Militarily Japan is a defeated nation but those of you who have listened closely to my speech or read the text will note that we have not surrendered. I and Japan simply agreed to abide by the requirements of the 'Potsdam' agreement. The occupation of Japan by the Americans will end. One day they will go home.

"The war is now economic."

"The Americans have demanded the disillusionment of the Chrysanthemum Throne and the execution of some of our best generals and politicians as a sop to the world. As from today the throne as you know it ceases to exist. Only myself, my wife and our children will be recognised and thus supported by the country. You must all make your own way in the world, without rank, without title and without money. You will all retain the land and houses you live in but that is all, all estates and additional houses must be given over."

"In recognition of all your work and the sacrifices you have made for the throne over these years, the Imperial Palace will be sympathetic to requests for funding for any businesses you engage in. We will use the proceeds of 'Golden Lily' to rebuild our cities and industries. The

Americans will help us to do this. They have used a terrible weapon on our country for no reason. We know this, they know this, but the world does not. The Americans have lied to the world. Your task now will be to lead the world in technology, electronics and industry. I expect this to be achieved within twenty years. We can afford to do this."

The soft gong sounded as he turned to go.

"What are you going to do Chichibu?" Former Prince Takeda asked his uncle as they walked together towards the waiting cars.

"Nothing. I'm too ill, too tired, all the killing keeps me awake at night. I drink tea at two in the morning and I'm falling asleep at nine. I feel like an old spent man Takeda. How about you? What are you going to do?"

"Retire to the ranch and breed horses. I want to create life, not end it."

"How's your sleeping?"

"Bad. Scared that I'm entering the blackness I condemned thousands to. Do you think it makes a difference if you kill one man or ten thousand men?"

"Don't know. I suppose it's like the soldier who fires one bullet aimed at the heart of a man he doesn't know and the airman who pressed the release button for the bomb on Nagasaki."

It was three thirty am, the air was cold but the air inside the stable seemed warm even though there was no heat.

Tsuneyoshi Takeda and his eldest son Tsunetada leant on the wooden rail of the stall looking at the mare . She was sitting in the dry straw pulling clumps of hay from the hanging net. Beside her was a newborn foal, barely two hours old but already up on his feet.

"He's beautiful father, look at him bouncing around like a spring."

Father and son were mesmerised by the absolute joy of this new clean life, shining, glistening, brand new eyes looking quickly everywhere. Looking at the warm air pushing out of his nostrils, looking at his mother, touching her, feeling her, drinking her milk then jumping away, trying out his legs to see what they could do.

"What shall we call him father? How about 'Blaze' he has a white blaze down his face."

"No Tsunetada, we'll call him 'Ben'. We'll call him Ben."

The End.

Printed in Poland
by Amazon Fulfillment
Poland Sp. z o.o., Wrocław